NO SEATBELTS–

SHE'S DRIVING AGAIN UNRESTRAINED

SARAH WILSON

iUniverse, Inc.
New York Bloomington

NO SEATBELTS -
SHE'S DRIVING AGAIN UNRESTRAINED

iUniverse books may be ordered through booksellers or by contacting:

iUniverse
1663 Liberty Drive
Bloomington, IN 47403
www.iuniverse.com
1-800-Authors (1-800-288-4677)

Because of the dynamic nature of the Internet, any Web addresses or links contained in this book may have changed since publication and may no longer be valid. This is a work of fiction. All of the characters, names, incidents, organizations, and dialogue in this novel are either the products of the author's imagination or are used fictitiously.

ISBN: 978-1-4401-2499-0 (pbk)
ISBN: 978-1-4401-2497-6 (cloth)
ISBN: 978-1-4401-2498-3 (ebk)

Printed in the United States of America

iUniverse rev. date: 2/18/09

I would like to dedicate this book in loving memory of my nephew,
Christopher Michael Todd
September 2, 1976 – October 29, 2006

My Prayer For The Future

Disguise delinquent youth's face
with sapphire heron wings,
until spirits blain Elysian Fields,

and heavens become part
of their coming glory,
as their appearance is recreated.

Clothe them in flecked tickcloth,
so billows can suckle
blithe minds, and calm their destructive frolics.

Shield them from splinter-glass,
so riches of passion,
happiness, clarity and excitement

mirror silver kindness,
as love felt devotions
sheet them in pure pelerines so they cross

the glad dreams of youth's spring,
calm as giddy rapture
pushes pungent difficulties away,

leaves virtue to shimmer,
and they'll get one more chance
gracefully as an Indian summer.

Live with passion, Sarah Wilson

No Seat Belts

It's July and dry heat wraps shocks.
Chrome-plated grills flash.
Her winking eyes tease day's speed,
moves west of Appalachia's chain.

Mile markers live fast lanes in black/white.
Apsaras speed with sky, shadow tire's slide;
lull complication of parent's departure,
asleep at the wheel paying no heed
to signs stirring wide-open spaces.

Times clump together where people spend
whole lives on plains as patched dirt
where ancestors once survived.
Princess is a hood ornament.

She steers car one-armed; emotions flee.
V-8 hums monotones as Cadillac floats,
suspends time where Ramblers once ruled.
She climbs with the sun, set free
from the whiteness of her breast.

Hurtles took hues of that morning
midday-tinted, beaten gold, tanned nude,
before she pretends to be a thing of light,
whose whipping wings would never still.

Parents impel yawns, stretch, comment,

"She's driving again unrestrained."

In the following pages you will find country thoughts of Sarah Wilson. She hopes the reader will find insight from her life for theirs. Her poetry and prose dives off her lips into the reader's soul.

*** The front and back covers are pictures of Sarah Wilson as a child. ***

After 50 --

My husband and I moved to Leesville,
South Carolina in 2006 –
because it's dazzling, alien, and countrified.
Our lives began again in a garden of color,
where the daystar came to our souls
dressed in yellow spitting its fiery blood;
the rain fell, fragrant, from corpulent clouds.
Strange music uplifts us in a rainbow nisus
as the creator paints multi-colored designs.
Hard believed destiny delivers us
to this edge
to begin life again,
to be born again,
to seep as water might
in a smokescreen of dazzling mist,
and shimmering trees.

Our minds introduced to change
turn us back into students. We came first
with our oldest, then she grew distant,
now we're alone.

We spend much of our time reviewing our lives.
After raising four children, and eight grandchildren
later,
the sand and sun glitters muted shades,
and red hawks fly our way.

I'm the free spirit, daydreamer,
and small town girl that studies squalls.
Clearly, we came here not only as students,
but as escapees.

Memories are visuals
like the hypnotic assault
of the prettiest rainbow
you've ever seen.

Ribs of color whirl stars
and kingdoms of freshness rise
to the crimson light of a setting sun.

When I met Roger he'd already been killed,
a couple of dozen times,
once for every year he'd been alive.
He didn't have a mouth, but I did.
I remember telling him there had to be something
he wanted to do with his life.

He told me he wanted to live in Mexico,
at the edge of the border with me,
and raise children and taco dogs,
have a greenhouse garden:
chilies, tomatoes, beans, corn,
and a little plot of weed.

We'd earn our living taking legals back and forth,
shun the world of retail, Internet,
and indoor plumbing.
There'd be no TV,
and in the winter months festive lights would paint
our sky. The children could run half-wild,
chase the tumbleweeds,
and learn to play ball with prickly pears.

In those days he could do no wrong,
and had a way to make me weak-kneed,
and intensely hopeful.
He had too-large eyes with rings
of brilliant brown

wrapped around a green pupil.
I was as attentive as a child
engrossed in play.

After his D.W.I.
any mention of Mexico gelled
in disgust of hindsight.
Something Dad always said was 20/20.
I'd yell back that our children
would be throwing cactus
amid piles of dog turds,
and about the way our luck ran
we'd not even be able
to give away half-breed, six-toed dogs.
I almost packed up and left.

But he kissed ass like a pro,
and should have been an acrobat.
This mind-set spills out his frame.

Since then we've walked
marsh edges,
and shorelines,
collected shells,
and learned about different plant species.

I write about these subjects to console myself,
highlighting what I chose. Each year teaches me
how sand shifts, and widens craters overnight,
reminds me of both its frailty and its difference
from greener North Carolina grasses.

You are never far from nature here –
throaty squirrel's chatter,
temperamental birds
and the settling bed of sand.
Solitude is a striking snake that has laid low,

listened to pounds of tracking feet.
Not at all like your lover's thigh next to yours,
the adagio of panting breath,
the thumps and rustles that wake dawn
to someone's rising,
comforting heartbeats
of a life together.

We're two pine trees grafted
to each other,
a knuckle-like knot at eye level
where clouds flicker eerie,
shake keys of air,
and laugh hysterically.

The inflamed and fiercely contorted trees
of old apple orchards spook me.
Damaged limbs spread white lace,
cold fire in spring, and mix odor of blossoms,
ghostly and sweet. As I stand beneath
foreign canopies of South Carolina that hum,
and shake with green, I hear voices,
but I do not understand them.
Going out for me is opening my door,
and walking across the yard.
Roadside sits surrounded by trees,
thick plumes of pampas grass,
jets of monkey sod,
and banks of althea.

In time the outdoor growth moves inside.
Celebratory seasons dazzle green.
North Carolina Mountains roll somersaults,
and everywhere there were sounds of water.
In South Carolina I've not gotten use to quiet.

Now I like living behind chained shadows,

colors that ring town. Crepe Myrtles, azaleas.

The earth leaves the air in patches,
a fresh cotton smell.
I long for simpler things,
and it sounds crazy for me
to throw myself at the South Carolina sky.
My father always told me you could take the girl
out of the mountains, but not the mountains
out of the girl, as if the dead still had claims
they'd impose.

I saw a bobcat today.
It leaped the dirt road, one long bound,
seemed strangely small, its tail thick,
the color of dung.

Gentle rolls of blueberries reenter
the view, sponginess of South Carolina
sand between my toes.

I walk on, elated, and curiously composed.
Every moment tightly holds my white
double crown tilted upward against
blue sky.

Anxious, the bobcat follows,
his injured smell lingers.
This odor and loose change jiggles,
horse-shaped clouds saddle my back
to senses; breakfast should be ready.

In June 2007, an extraordinary day engaged
myself and daughter, Penny.
We traveled to Blueberry Road,
and faced walls of blueberry bushes.
Rich blue-to-black balls

planted in sand,
marked by red flags
depict areas we could pick.
$1.00 a pound,
but I remember telling Penny
they couldn't weigh the ones we ate.

On the first row, rain had washed
the blue wonders clean.
Wet bushes rattled wind;
at the edge daisies twitched,
and ladybugs crawled.

I followed the row, gradually sloping round.
A bee buzzed my face and veered off,
stopping at a point where a small stake glowed red.
Here we were strapped, buckets half full
in running battles of who could pick the most.
Standing there a painted memory of how
my ancestors must have gathered food.
It was my Indian heritage in overdrive.

Twenty three pounds later my mother's happy,
but I knew that, far from the painting, I'd merely
sketched the day. As a writer I've felt the limits
of time and know my ability to see and record
for my own future generations.

Blueberries, round and sweet,
how we'd roll them under our tongue,
eating half before Grandmother covered them.

Sugar and milk swam with small brown parts,
floated to the top.
I'd poise them on a large soupspoon,
until they would be gone,
then dive to the bottom

of the bowl for sunken treasures
of sugar and love.
Of course Penny wasn't born then.

I read her beautiful frown,
wishing alive her great-grandmother.
With fried hoecake bread for breakfast,
wishing back her creosol dream house;
it was sold to strangers in her passing.

My daughter never knew her,
but she sat around edges
wrapped up in soft colored afghans,
hardbound books on her lap.
We splash-flipped at her feet,
provoking denizen of deep,
overshadowing her river.

We trickled on home's staircase,
eager for towels.

Always with ankles delicately crossed,
always with something dainty in lap,
she worked her knitting needles
with still hands, while playing war
at the foot of her rocker. I tripped
around her clumsy social graces.

She died while everyone picked blueberries.
Spring sunshine danced in dust sparkles
above the table. My eyes watched
Mother press a hand to her cheek and cry
into the telephone. I didn't feel the sting
of broken glass dropped in slow motion
meeting my feet and the floor.

Locked in with myself in a bedroom,

crying against the window,
my eyes left to follow clouds
that Grandmother ascended toward.
Her new home was in blueberry colors.

Will Penny will ever know
the secrets my heart holds,
like one knows from the pull of gravity
when your heart falls to the ground?

Look past sadness, and anger.
Roger and I stand in lines of devastation,
greed, starvation, and violence.
Desperately, we grab for brass rings,
learn how little we really know,
and find the very ones we trust damage us.

Love is the first day of sun,
after a winter of snow,
a secret thicket
of blueberries up your drive.
Love is how you are born,
and something that can ruin your life.

This is the start of the sweet,
and hungry taste
of life living overgrown
on sand hills of forever.

Our oldest asked me for help, and just for kicks
Roger tagged along. That morning things
disappeared (supposedly), and we both learned
how little our trust was valued.
In addition to disappearing acts,
I was accused of multiple other sins.
Have you ever been there?
My oldest is a person,

who always wants to leave
wherever she is.
She tells me she's just like me.
Tea colored she once bloomed,
Like sassafras in the fields -
Now, her branches are bare.
Moods moved by the wind,
Deer escape hunter's sunrise,
Fracas composes song.
Promise of return
Before winter claims lone limbs
The frost is still chilled.
Thunder in the plains
Casts delicate veil of rain,
Weeping longs the lost.
In these moments, I realize closeness unspoken
proves time really has no power to change zilch.
We don't understand, and now study humble
relationships between children and parents.

We are the prey that replaces their wildness.
This diminished trust withdraws any comfort
we'd felt. We are nothing, but cow ants
trying to survive.

Something invasive has changed our landscape.
Maybe, I should stop praying,
so absurdly, for things that teach us once again
about loss and the survival instincts of renewal.

We've arrived amid bare rooms, rumpled smiles
from stained people. Roger reclines,
his shirts and jeans have turned the color
of sand. I write my poetry in chunks,
and splashes of disaster.

He's a man on his back, lying stiff,

resistance worn,
a bed board being taken apart.
Sparklers twirl.
Hints of the 4th of July
touch down.

We've found ourselves
when first flushes of roses bleed
into the west, study brick-a-bract clouds,
their rows spitting out posses.
I think black squirrels have it better than us,
they build their nests in high branches,
where in spring they hide
in sweet-smelling masses,
nothing to disturb them
except cool trickles of breeze.

But I'm just a squawking parrot,
green in a blue sky,
where my children flame fires,
walk over me, and are no longer balanced
on my hip.

My ancestors collected bubbles,
moonshine to wash over pain.
I have none, but v-shaped pills
that winks my brain to numbness.
In shadows of family feuds
my face hangs at dusk, stares
past fence lines, up hills.

Even after I go to bed
these thoughts return by dawn.
The shove finally stills,
and I sleep a few hours.

Our dwelling in suffocating shade

among twisted oaks strip thoughts,
sand widens the sun-grinded edge.

I squat between dreams without the benefit
of guns or prayer,
and can only watch heat lightning
whip the sky; rain slices bare arms
in stretched, jagged shivers.

In the broken phrases of life,
it's unclear whether sand drifts here,
gorges mute with treetops and sorrow.

Perhaps, it's the fierce cry of mourning,
hurrying south under our oldest fear
rapidly forming, and dissolving clouds,
leaving manic steps
stone-carved in cold muller.

Change is everything and everywhere.
Mid-year and dog days rain late;
mucked sand roads ignite the cooler mums.

And on the South Edisto, logs float by us
in syrupy air, but gallop fast-steed speed
through hip-high basil, and gawky bramble
scatters black squirrels erupting from dust,
and sunlight.

This is our great retirement.
This muscled sprawl of grandchildren
slips in sand.

Their pet pig, four hundred pounds,
lifts his hooves, circles my view,
holds my violet eyes in his flat yellow stare.

I think his carcass might fill the hole
my Chrysler sinks in.

Three feet past my porch
the sand slopes root
of the squat Easter Egg bush,
clutches flatland,
and yellow Easter eggs go uncollected.

My grandson is up the hill
on his belly, awaits my return inside,
runs down, cackles, picks the first egg,
then a second,
throws them against the house,
only, to find it does not crack yolk.
Roger and I are joined like earthworms
watching him run back home.

By noon, Dominick hens and Rhode Island Reds
will cluck songs. They peck at what grass seed I've
strewn,
and I'll write poems that blister your heart.

We were told this area is dangerous –
Charles Town -- where the sun sets in the south,
and the morning fog is thick as mushroom soup,
warm and only rare breezes refresh sweaty skin.

Perhaps this is peace; or the sand drifts bare truths;
or God, that gargle on the red tip of your tongue.

The hours of coolness in a.m. bring relief.
It's still November, and warm, and humid,
Temperatures in the high eighties, air motionless,
and heavy with the threat of rain.

We have a rural mailbox

with a delivery person that brings
the outside world to our door.
Even though Roger has to find it,
and put it back up each morning.
How can unknown people cause such disturbances
to older people that have more to do than one would
expect?

But all birds have to sing out at intervals.
We have to put place and time in perspective.
It depends on how you gaze out the window.
Some see seas of shining green,
some spot dark hues that furl leaves inward.

Our land is uniformed with caps
of forest leafed out, needles that color the scene.
The best time of day is at night
beneath a canopy of stars.
Recent meteor showers spray
delicate light in the center of our universe.

My lookout spot is a metal chair
two small dogs often rest in,
and I stare them down for the spot.
The chair seems to sit on an edge
where sunlight has walked off the ledge.
No brittle limbs could amble the massive thickness
left by dark. Remember openings are only
temporary.

Even though sun comes a little earlier in the fall,
and stays up a little later in the spring
mankind has to shade his own growth,
and seize shelter under a parasol
of his own making.

I walk the length of my driveway, 1,200 feet,

put up a new mailbox my good neighbor
(the one on the right side) provides.

We paint the numbers against the red,
and by the time my husband walks
down the hill bringing the mail to me
our mailbox has been stolen again.

Our neighbors on the left side stay home,
watch TV, scratch powerball tickets,
and eat frozen dinners bought with food stamps.
They sit around a bonfire at night, shoot guns,
then call the three-year-old police department
to report sightings of clouds
in the shape of Jesus shooting through the sky.

Cumulus clouds move south on a quiet wind,
twelve degrees cooler than yesterday's dawn.
I lean forward to rest my arm on the chair,
begin taking in details of the moment in this light,
the country stirs.

Irregular rattle-tap-tap sprinkles tin,
somewhere in the crawlspace,
as though, mice rock back,
and forth holding an empty cup.

A copperhead blends
into the muscadine,
snakes closer,
on a Sunday morning
where heathens flesh out
faith pushing the plate.

Sadness is the loneliest kind
of bad weather,
it's more like lightning than rain,
because it only strikes a person

who least suspects it.
Leesville presents an interesting pattern
of human life.

Red hawks begin their regular patrol
at six thirty. The chickens squawk by seven.
The emergence of eight grandchildren
outrun the yellow bus.

My husbands nods his head, spends
the whole day walking back and forth,
either struggling with whether to shovel
sand from one place to another,
fill pock holes, or visit
our right side neighbor.
He climbs the hilltop, and I watch his progress.
A bird flies, lands atop a branch,
his wing and tail feathers spread,
beautiful bluish sheen,
a few wispy tufts of white down
blaze his breast.
Like Roger the bird's clumsy,
but already a dodger.

Both peer with steely blues,
preen and stretch often.
The bird pokes the leaves,
sticks and browning grass,
and Roger duplicates the same actions
with his walking stick.

Glints of their eyes keep me alert.
Stomach growls murmur to my brain's center.
Without prompting both follow me back home.
Our eyes lock silent, and soon smells
of corn beef hash and eggs overpower us.
Scent awakes all birds
to a wild melee of song.

Symphony or feasts all are revived.

Red maples tinge orange, colors surge,
and cool air spreads relief.
Here we stand mono-colored miniatures
of life.

Beneath the canopy of fall we remain
the only domesticated variety.
Striking against spectacles
of the myriad --
knotty needles stare back.

Like the clamor for food
ear-shattering quiet surrounds us,
closes in the bare edge of sunset.
I think openings are always temporary,
whether it is the woods rushing in
or our climbs to escape.

We survive under an umbrella
of cones.

Our old homestead is only visible
when the green dies,
and unbroken vines shed.

In springtime you see kudzu coveting ground,
where flatlanders once plowed fields.
Purple violets sprout,
and what my grandfather once called seven sisters
(a type of wild rose)
reminds me of how valuable space can be.

The people that once lived here are scattered
under gravestones in tiny cemeteries.
Weather has erased their names.

Maybe it is a good thing,
as some dates reflect sad truths.

Just below the lookout to the south
steep granite drop-offs cascade water. Runoffs,
the ones that gnaw scars into your heart.
A few hundred feet below horseshoes turn.
You can't see them from here,
but screeching brakes tell the tale.
In this neck of woods even relatives associate
in split clans, according to land they inhabit.

This area seems alive to me,
as my own family traces
our edge of home.

Who knows, twenty-some-odd years from now
it may only be prime deer pasture.
If I had it to do over again,
I'd buy open land and plant fields,
maybe blueberries, harvest friendships
of many generations to follow.

Steely blues land on a tree,
similar to one,
where my son and his friend built
a clubhouse – one that hasn't seen
children in so many years.
Birds fly in and out windows,
raise their broods
in mud nests.

A lot of what exists in these woods
remains naked to the common person.
Most lives go unnoticed, seldom
do we leave records, only bits and pieces,
Maybe what you might call dots.

How many wish to connect the dots?

Think of how beautiful birds conceal their young.

And we are the sleepwalkers
that do not recognize the songs they sing.

I hurtle back the other way,
in exaggerated emotion.
My eyes drive freehand,
in and out of clouds,
waiting to be scooped up,
and hauled off.

Dinnertime arrives, and we are briefly animated,
deciding about an energy bar or protein drink.
Wheat colored light puddles the room.
Pale violet shades into apricot yellow
until sunset patterns glint wires,
drop color on two rows
of azaleas we've planted.
Day to night this pattern hardly varies.

I watch with fickleness the diurnal rhythm
which my oldest offers in events
of unpredictability.

A beer-bottle mosaic paves the path.
She's made a promise to begin praying again,
as soon as she's not so desperate.

Promises are many,
as prayer invokes visions
of the all mighty down on his knees,
hands clasped tight over hers.
Tears of fear and loss are there.
She's not willing to commit.

It's the degradation of having to imply
the only sense she has is when
she's down on her luck
cursing a God for wanting
a more normal life.

I watch with unquenchable fascination.
If I could lean out as far as dared
it would be in the other direction.

My desire is to study red cardinals,
the brown sparrow,
whip-o-wills in flight.
Their aggressive calls stall me,
and I rarely leave, become a tourist
to their world.

The tortoise pace of day parallels
my husband's peeved amble
with wide-flung strides.
He's become rotund,
and oblivious to our disruptions.
I'm a boulder in his creek.

Roger wears overalls, white sneakers,
sand and spit shines their earthly glow.
He wears his dollar clothes
that reveal how I like to shop His House,
a favorite thrift store.

My husband is a slave to moods,
lost in self-indulgence,
but he stands tall and skips moments
of awkwardness. Vaguely, I wonder
if something is wrong with his clothes,
and fancy him freshly shaved.

I'm fascinated by glib comments,
the mad jig and his constant gripe.
He has a mean hip
that swings temperamental.

My first marriage was the North Pole,
the second a pervert,
and Roger is the South Pole,
and I'm stuck on the divided line,
trying to navigate
the children in between.
I think, maybe, I'm dysfunctional,
incited by riots of the heart.

Going back to my second husband;
he stole women's bras,
strapped them around cut off stumps.

I remember finding them under a full moon.
They looked like headless nymphs wearing c,
d and double-d cups on display.

He clasped his hands to the hem
of his tight t-shirt,
lifted it to the sky,
and tossed it aside.

I crossed my arms,
and for some reason I thought of slingshots.
On this day my voice was wrong,
a lemon on a peach tree.

When confronting him
his silence was heavy,
like a cloud of smoke that follows
a hydrogen bomb.
Minute shyness breaks out,

and everyone walks in circles.

All this gaits together with kindred modulations,
seems mysteriously revealing.
Lingering we embrace,
separate with resolve,
then embrace once more.
Afternoon halts us,
turns us toward each other
in sidesplitting laughter.
I think I'll probably never see
such things again.

My son lives his life in flames.
His life in flames.
One day he is going to start a fire,
and I'm not going to be able to put it out.

Tom's the funny kid, the funny kid always has
something wrong.
That's why he's funny, always jerks people's minds to
other places.

He argues with me and I tell him
I'd never agree with the life he lives,
at least probably not until I wear diapers again,
and only then if he was in charge of changing them.

Along with my oldest deranged daughter,
my son has disappeared.
I'm fed in wordless ways.

Another sort of animation draws me,
the sound of thunder,
rising hisses snake treetops,
make my eyes drift upward
to follow the skyline.

With impossible slowness,
there is a sudden dimming
of sunlight, and I run,
watch the slant of rods
from a silent rain.

Fifty is going to bed early,
wishing I could wake up
with a new face, or better yet,
get a new life without children
that only speaks in tongues of green.

Because of this I'm always on the prowl
for chaos. In a few days I'll get a letter
from my lost son,
opening line always being, "It's Tom."

The letter keeps reading itself
shatters glass bearing my wits,
holds blue goblets that never spill drops.

Memories become pain;
pain becomes mental unrest,
bars that should hold criminals.

I have a thing about jailbirds,
it seems like they'll do anything
to hide their heart.

The Indian in Tom makes him mean,
and when he drinks, it places him
with other unhappy people.

My mother says he can't help it.
Meanness is a song in our family,
that passes from one generation
to the next.

Even as a child Tom cultivated his reputation,
first as a delinquent,
and second as a possible drug user.
His narcotic terror numbs me.

The words might change,
but the melody doesn't.

She sits on her wrap-a round porch,
plunked in the middle of nowhere,
and tells me, "Yes,
heartache is an Indian's middle name",
and adds, "I don't know all the answers."

I look at the sky-reaching double clusters
of pink and white Cosmos,
and she blinks, "There's more."
She points out the pine, for instance,
says to lose my sight in the bark,
listen for the black squirrels clatter,
and that I'll hear them sing at night.

And then there are all the old sayings
about what her mother said to her.

Then her soul soars
to the cratered moon and back,
and to this day I think I could sit
with her forever.

If she's hoeing hills with a vengeance,
I'll sit on the ground.
Sometimes if the day's swallowed me whole,
I'll rest my heart in her lap, like a child.

Mama's shoulders lift and shake serene,
her face moves the sun.

For the first time I actually see
how pretty, unlined, and youthful
her soul is. Her lips are thin,
but clearly defined,
the way a tulip shapes,
and her hair streaked
black as Greek olives,
and pigmented red.

As for me, the dance is halfway over,
and I'm teetering on the edge
of a swamp,
like a sow's ear waiting to be turned
into a silk purse,
something worth putting money into,
and I tell myself someday
someone will reap riches on me.
Until then I'll wait.

I don't know how to say it
other than everything turns upside down,
like a turtle on its back
that can't get up again.

Rainwater courses in sheets,
down the calico-patched grass
we've managed to grow.
No matter how wild the weather
I feel comforted.
My back turns away family,
east and west,
the land I share rattle-drums hail.

And from the pane I see marvels,
the light's affair, glinted bits of mica
in the façade of the future.
Beneath the summer storm,
our dwelling seems secure,

and a single mind dances ballroom
with a male mannequin
in black tuxedo.
He moves like a float in a parade.

Morning pleads tones
of erotic petulance.

I hum, step beats
to the piano clock,
wait for Jesus.

Tramp moon trespasses
into my past, stirs up
Valentine's Day.
On this day, I remember
how Roger never failed
to make me mad.
Jaw stiffens, breaks angry,
moves outside and rakes the yard.
As a result our grass was always combed.

I've always thought we fussed
to make up.

One year I turned so mad,
I made something beautiful: Calla.
She's my good child.
Her beat sustains me,
flowery, remorseless,
a mysterious statement,
nothing can touch her.

But now, Roger makes me feel
I'm going to burst
by neglect of cards and candy.
So, I do. Bits of me dance dark
to the tunes of a two-timing Jesus.

I wonder if he'll ever know
the secrets my heart holds
like others know from the pull
of gravity when one's heart
falls to the ground.

Today I'm glad for the change of weather.
I feel wind, moving gray clouds,
more so, than I could feel before;
The walk up the driveway would be cooler.
I'd daydreamed in my chair for hours
when my husband came outside.
The faint odors in the breeze change,
dampen the acrid smell of marigolds.
He pauses, speechless.
He wants to lead a normal life,
but the stroke prevents that.
In his eyes is a stunned, hopeless daze.
Light appears obscured and diminished.

Every other day Roger tells me
to take him up the street,
drop him and his money off
at the rest home.

I tell him men are like stars,
and they fill the sky,
and that the river is full of fish,
and maybe if he'd fish for a new one,
he'd stop being so cranky all the time.

He said he didn't know
about the men being stars,
but I might be right about the fish.

Roger might be an awesome kisser,
but that doesn't keep him
from being a total ass.

The muted tones I see in his clothes fade,
stir the new day's dust.
A flock of red hawks give chase
to the chickens. Another end.

My want is to stay in this moment,
but I know I've spent all the time
that has been offered right now.
The passion my husband imbibes
seems profound,
and almost unfathomable.
I stare at his huge hands,
which I want to touch.
The stillness is unbelievable.

Funny, how the things
you dream for you never get,
and the nightmares
you don't want
you always find.

Mankind seems incredible,
and amazingly alien.
Precision and orderliness
of perception lifts me out of my chair.
He's given me thoughts of how to grasp it all.
I think this is an epiphany.

We stare for many minutes,
and my steps are toward the bushes.
The moment my knees touch flowers,
my fingers peel bark.
My double crown stills,
touches the melancholy sky.

Déjà vu turns, throws me into the past,
I'm ten, chasing lightning bugs,
the mason jars tumble;
my friends are light footed as doe,
at the fence line I've long forgotten.

I see faces in the traces of sky,
boys chasing girls,
and I see Roger and I see myself.
My hopes are the trees will never obscure
the view to heaven.

Sometimes my mind wanders
to the cove where my father,
and all of his brood attended school
in a tiny one-room schoolhouse,
now converted
to a small and very private chapel.
I see the birds that enter its roof vents and nest.

We've no memories like this in Leesville.

A lot of what exists in my mind can't be seen
from my chair.

Deciphering natives from the woods
where we live is like trying
to comprehend the landscape
without a map.

One neighbor's a retired wildcat.
She took early lovers,
rode Pelion on a Harley,
while she was high
on pot or worse.
Now at twenty plus

she's reached a plateau,
known otherwise as compromise.
She's engaged to someone boring,
and she's struggling to make him more.

She's got the woman's walk –
neither the swagger of a tomboy
nor the watch-me-roll of a sexpot,
but the straight-hipped authority
of a grown up sexual woman.

She lets out the peal of wild laughter;
this is the signature tune
of humorless people.

The birds and trees we know better –
at least we can call them by their names.
With this thought comes a sense of joy,
which I take to breakfast.

Roger was once a distance runner,
but lately, it takes him most of the morning
to pace the path to the outside world.
I travel behind him
with my doldrums taking on his stride.
He stops often and I think road kill,
or he picks at the gooseberries.

I'm a crow picking his habits.

When he stoops over
to pick up a beer can
my mind jogs down the path
of what other observers that watch us must think –
he's walking under the influence.

He's not dwelling on their opinion,
only on the nickel the can will bring.

Early the following morning,
I realize my husband has lost
the advantage of surprise.

He's Cherokee and meant to be a scout,
but my Mother can't remember
whether I'm Black Foot or Shoshone.

I'm only a fraction Indian;
truth being we're all mixed up.
Pride is a game none of us should play.

I'm bogged down in heavy snow,
like the one in Franklin,
where I walked three miles to work,
later sent home after an hour.
Today we'll be in hand-to-hand combat
with an old lawn mower.

After the cut we water the grass,
a simple gesture of respect.
I let the water run through my tips,
slowly, watch the small green
spikelets lift, teeter in the warm air.

Second pauses bring me
to watch a new nest of cow ants.
When first spotted I'd just known
I'd discovered a new species.
Too much TV. Reminds me of watching
all the underwater species,
newly discovered,
that has been altered
by chemical dumps.

I captured some of the cow ants
in a mason jar,
placed sand and holes in the jar,
planned on taking them
to the agricultural office,
but fifteen minutes later
they go belly-up.

Roger calls me a bug murderer,
flushes them down the toilet,
their red bodies spiral, and blur.

Goosebumps rise on my arms.

He'd never be tall,
and I'd never be decisive,
always the one left standing
in between, easily spellbound.

A spanking freshness erupts the air,
encourages long thoughts,
remembers a kind of sweetness
that creates independent people.
A silent funk falls about our home,
suddenly, a photograph appears.

It was of a young girl riding a pretty pony.
My adopted cousin, whom
I always thought was so much luckier
than me, until, her circumstances revealed
a sadder situation delivering her
to where she was.

Her face was relaxed,
waved off my anxiousness.
I'm glad she visited my backyard today.
I continue to watch the cow ants.

Promises are made to me
that I'll return to yesterday, and try
to find what has been lost to me.
This world has always been a widow,
and widower, the one we leave bereft
when we slip into the past.
Now what has always seemed true
is no longer true.

I want to lie down and swim in the shade
overrun with emptiness,
but I love this life,
want it to cradle me longer.

Like seeds propelled toward a future field,
when the wind licks the treetops,
I walk in the perfumed day,
lie with views beneath the cool roots,
sprout images tangled and damned.
What will happen to the soul in me?

I'm fed on these scenes,
which I fear will go on living
after Roger dies,
and realize how a tree must feel,
when, unexpectedly,
vines seize past the layers of bark
to a deeper place,
where sap stops to flow.

A skein of wind is caught
in the needle knots;
rigor mortis hangs a black squirrel
backside up. Roger squats naked
atop a stump, anus aimed
at the same number of years he is.

He might scratch his butt,
and feel as old as the tree,
but when he spots poison ivy
his brain responds.

Greedy for safety,
he pulls up his jeans,
and escapes all the crap.

Slats of sand happen to push up
through the smell of honeysuckle.
Salt air smells wet and moldy wood,
and the rotting guts of a brim fish.
On TV gulls whine, kids squeal,
and sharks splash the tide.

Skin tingles from yesterday's sunburn.
Green tea insinuates the idea of health,
although, I live in despair.
You have to love this fragile land.
Is it fascination to watch something
beautiful die?

Urges fight me to put down the ink,
and go outside
where the western staircase
rolls out its crinoline,
floats on the South Edisto River
of September.

Before me the wooly canopy
of pasture holds my nostrils close
to the cryptic stench of earth,
where the King's Crown shimmers,
shoots up in the dew,
amid a pine bark haven.

I'd rather watch the queens
work the wildflowers
than trail the dull tracks
wherever it is they go.

My soul shouts words are whips,
and wedge open the sky-colored flowers,
permits the flayed stems to utter
what the truth is.

I'd rather listen to the water,
its words always muddled,
just out of earshot.

It's not the words themselves
that jolts the soul,
but their absurd flash,
the same one pallbearers follow,
first to the funeral home,
then to the graveside.

If I was scripting my own death,
I'd know how to make the chafe and cane
of the September field take on that gist,
and I'd rest for a bit in the image
of my body wedded to the black
bacteria, beloved dirt, and the dash
the weed seeds send away,
their slim filaments of sprout.

But it's not my death that's set.
It's the earths upon whose body I lie,
and toward whom the cow ants trace.
The earth has been crying its goodbyes.
Another world will soon appear,
but I love this one.

I've let it hug me longer than I should.
Can you imagine what will happen
to my soul, which I fear will live on
after this loved world dies?

The mail delivers news from my son, Thomas.
He's escaped again, only to be locked away.
Aiken's twenty plus miles from here,
and his salutation "Mom, It's Tom" resonates.
Secretly, this amuses me.
I'm awestruck in wonder
of how mental illness handles the heart.

Roger and I glare,
hunch over his palette of words.
Freud reminds me about cast-offs,
how they can sweep in,
and seize your nerves.
He's no longer a boy,
but a man that makes distorted choices,
choosing the company
of ones who'll only converse
with him in drunken moments.

Pros and cons separate intelligence.
He's married to bonds of jail,
amazes me with frantic details.
Alcohol is his touchstone of power,
it inebriates popularity,
persists a desire to break
the Guinness Book of World Records.

How many times can he have intense affairs
with an old crock?

I think if one can't be a great poet,
then why not be a great criminal.

I'm feeling age, sigh rare cameos
of betrayal—
teeter the edge.

Legs turn, search for sunlight.
Memories arrive, outline the heart's sink
to whisper.

We speak and skirt the truth,
the sad circles,
prowl perimeters,
and make small jokes.

We have to do this,
and drown in numbers
that might as well be tattooed
to our foreheads at birth.
Numbers become labels,
twisters that plummet low.

I'm not complaining,
as I generally follow the gist of rules.
The trick to being different is
to be understood.

I hear hammering nails.
You'd think we lived next to a coffin maker
after a plague. When I try to sleep
the hammers start again.

Maybe,
I need to go to a sleep deprivation program.

Finally, at night we dream,
and cry for what we've lost.
The next day is always a new twist.

Chickens lunch in gay parties,
gaze gently over grass seed.
I think fried chicken.
A dark-feathered beauty struts,
half-grasps me to step forward.
In what seem seconds dusk ripples,
and enthusiasm grows weary.
This exhaustion awaits a new day.

Roger's learned to control the cow ants with telepathy,
he sends them in hordes to battle me.

But I fix him,
pull out my mason jar,
scoop them up like turds in a toilet,
and smother them in molasses
so he'll enjoy them with his 3:00 tea.

I've wondered if they can telepathically relay
their mental anguish from his cavity.

Surely the sun will go down soon.
Sweat pours from every pore,
and the smell is ripe,
like sour grapes and overturned dirt,
and wait for an evening shower that probably won't come,
and won't last long if it does.

Later in the evening topped pines,
blacked cutouts, etch across a sky color
of dying embers.

This place has a too-quiet abandoned feel.

Leesville runs along the highway
past Pelion, pronounced by locals

as "Peeing", I was told to drop the "I".
Pelion has turned out to be the way
to everywhere.

We have a small white house
with gray trim.
There is a large front yard
with too many azaleas —
too many places to hide.

The reason for azaleas is they grow,
where grass doesn't, and sold cheap
at the local IGA. $2.00 a bucket
come spring or fall.

I keep respectful distances from town,
except for the Peach Festival in Gilbert,
or the once a year Peanut Festival.

Every day we drive just to watch
the streets, four corner stores
at one intersection,
people heavy with armloads.
They walk tall and straight and easy.
Eyes travel past the windshield,
straight into the sun,
a golden hole punched through the sky,
a bright and brutal spotlight pointed on my face.

Our plot is lowland flat, a nose-dive that cooks
under the sun, lines my face, and anything
we try to grow.

Gardening is something I've done all my life.
Even as a child, I planted seeds,
sucked grape pits down to the tiniest strings,
and planted them on the gully's edge.
Even planted rotten apples, peach pits, potato eyes,
and I grew all these plants in unlikely places.

Roger walks back and forth,
in and out of my head.
I watch him in this foreign land.
At the mailbox he looks
for something he's lost.
His hair blows, crosses his face,
and he pulls it back
with one hand.

Since we moved here
he's thinner and older, but –
Dammit – it has all been to his favor.
Like weathered wood: sun-cured,
but out of the rain,
where the knotty pines turn deep green,
and air blisters gold against grainy sky.

His skin has darkened,
yet, it seems half translucent.
I shake and hear his funny laughs.

This past winter I watched him walk
through snow to the mailbox, Minnie,
our light brown Chihuahua in toe.

Yesterday I spied on him
pulling the lawnmower cord,
squatting to prime the motor,
stretched backward to pull the handle.

He has strong shoulders and large hands.
His profile follows perfect lines from his nose
to his feet. The stroke has worn him down,
but I need to pretend,
and not pretend at the same time,
and do it well enough to fool him,
and myself both.

I tell lies,
stand on the porch,
say something
like how manicured the lawn looks,
overlooking the uncut overgrowth.

We want to be like any other two,
conversing subjects the other knows,
with one answering, all of it with
a plain pig-in-the-mud-sense
to every word, pitch,
and catch of the eye.

Ideals can be limiting.
Bee stings,
or trivia makes me feel trapped.
I know I need love too,
flowing tenderness
of fingers,
toes,
a tongue
along the earlobe.

I tell myself we are normal,
he doesn't get lost,
stumbles around,
and lives in my head,
just like he did thirty something years ago.
Who could lie to someone
they've loved thirty plus years?

I inherit drowsy days,
wake in first flush of feeling
the world belongs to me.
I'm dressed in delicacy,
unfussy clothes.

The trees small talk,
measure me barren.
I'm a gardener,
prune the limbs
to produce
one perfect picture.

Today the hunt is for smiles.
I put on cotton gloves that will not
allow my hands to yellow and crack.
Roger holds his cold hand around
my heart and tells me I'm a wolf in
sheep's clothing.

I say it takes one to know one.
There's the smile.
Some smiles are poison traps,
at least that is what I've been told.

Knocks against the trees gather attention,
Woodpeckers search for food. Beaks
predator-call and I wish they'd eat
cow ants.

In my starved garden
I pull out all the weeds,
and there they are (these ants),
pressed up at the top
where they've tried to get out,
to get to this bitch. Any that scurry
I stomp. It does not hurt them.

There's little cactus in bloom, prickly pear,
half-rose colored balls. One cactus
has five blooms, but you'd better not
put your nose close.
Their stickers go skin-deep,

have to fester outward.
The sky is so damn blue I want
to holler. We mosey up the drive,
and I show Roger gooseberries.
They are tiny bushes,
tight with blue-gray leaves,
like blueberry's foliage,
and a bright crown of blue bulbs.
They're earlier than the cactus,
so I poke around to find one,
under the shade of brown,
that's still in good color.

Roger gurgles, just a little sound.
All order of things happen within me
to hear it. I'm finding out that all
I ever wanted was to be with him.
In the mountains the only berries
that grow are poke weed, purple-
stained balls that my sisters,
and I used to pitch at each other.
Chaotic groundwork.

Kudzu wraps trees, like logic,
swallows up what shrinks inside.
This is a jungle world,
wild and looming.

It's not long before I lose sight
of the slight path we've found,
and feel like Tarzan trying to climb knotted ropes,
and I swing with my arms,
and twist to get through the bush.

This day is a fire spun gold,
and its brilliance flickers clouds,
dissipates alongside rain
we've had for a week.

Sunflowers stand thirsty.
Sand sifts under toes,
and licks the fire,
haloed in pure flashes
of yellow light.

Newton's theory was one that
everything's made up of yellow
and blue-seaside color. These floras
are whole summers to themselves.
Uncountable clusters of stalk light.
South Carolina grows these plants
here in unfamiliar ways.

Think of them as slender legs
sprouted straight where scamp
edges lean into the land,
as if gravity invisibly works
to bring us all down.
Is it a human soul the scientist
discovered?

Sand ruts, plugs of grass,
and pliant outlines of craters
accommodate the rain
that curves this earth.
Every inch reclaims speechless woods.
We don't even live in shouting
distance of our neighbors.

Father told me of how the highway
at the old home place was above
the road, one lane and unpaved.
Now the house rests below asphalt.

He remembered the first airplane
to fly overhead, and sometimes
the memory he had is more vivid than
words I live by now.

Words people never speak anymore.
The same birds and flora encircle me.
I see them now that I'm worn out,
and ready to lie down in a final dream.

Today we'll drive to Batesburg,
a place littered with grape pickers –
some on the ground, some on ladders,
all Mexican with baskets,
which are slightly kidney-shaped,
so they'll fit snug beneath the chest
of strapped men.

When I smell the muscadine I feel
I'm almost home. In peak seasons
yellow jackets attack unmercifully,
but the pickers leave when rings meet.

People pick crops to sell by the road stand.
We've become deliberate customers
that buys by the bushel, better
than generous pounds. I think
how all the work is inside now.

Through the thick branches I see
every buried field, crop sharer home,
and acres and acres of produce.
Distracted we follow the graceful road.
I can't tell if early fall is an angel,
or dark demon hefting the fruit.

My friend, John, will come to buy glass
this morning. Daylight collectors
gather at marsh's edge. What I offer
is my need to be seen by a comrade,
to feel the past pass from my hands
to his. It might as well be the icy
moon melting in my palms.
Ring-shaped as lips, sharp as a knife;
the light bathes the imminent event.
The position of glass is for his view,
reveals how one collector to another
centerpieces so many years.
The room burns amber in anticipation
of the beautiful pieces he'll purchase.

When you reside in the construed world
of art, you turn into the exotic,
like a bougainvillea taught to spread,
and blossom into the body and soul
of a peacock. Exotic plumage turns
carnival, keeps roots roused
by early sun, and scattering chat
rambles into a thicket where similarity
erupts, and we try to hide.

John is a kind erosion –
red sand in twists of arabesque,
open sky, and reedy pastures.
He speaks, lovingly, of his wife,
a white steed dipping her neck –
enticed by swan looks.
I peek above the clouds,
envision her as a robust heart,
churning her passion and muscle
for the love of this man.

Friends are forever,
receptions of the heart.
We all know
a lifetime is not too long
to live as friends
with the faith,
and love God gives.
The closeness will spring
from eternal hopes,
and the joy we struggle to live in.

Ripples and ridges and hills recede
into shadows, and yet the wick
he has ignited still burns.
After his departure the trees flash
to gold, change and flame,
red as the apple, brisk as a lemon.

I rest, think of how heartwarming
company can be, reach across time,
knowing how we are both peacocks,
passionate and showy,
the way one can embrace what comes,
love it fully and set it free.
What is it people say, "Birds of a Feather..."?

There are days I've no fancy tales,
no spoiled ideals to get me through,
just migraine from speculation,
and a pair of swollen ankles.

The sun is white-hot,
because the clouds have drifted
somewhere else to play.

In this delusion,
I duck into a drugstore,

in the aspirin aisle,
where a white-headed,
withered woman feels
the air spray filled by helium
that leaks out the balloons.

Today has decided to be formal.
There's no shrill of hawk calls,
or chicken's cluck.
Eyes perch the porch,
and await the new day's emergence.
Daylight pulls up its sequined dress,
like a naughty girl
glitters yellow beads,
half crystal, half-misty,
and opens vibrant.

The bobcat lurks,
and I want to creep out of my body,
aware both of our tails are bushed.

A clock always ticks,
voices take over my mind,
I cannot make them leave,
and they rasp the air.
Old words sit on lush velvet
grouped near marble,
elevate upturned smile.
Old eyes still wrinkle.
What does it mean these voices hidden
in poetry?

I speak and these words
repeat my words,
I raise my wet fist,
and they raise theirs
in retreat.

Roger needs to quit calling
the voodoo priestess, who takes cash
only at night, giving little spirit
to dead people before they surface,
and tells him
how he needs to quit loving
flying stuntwomen. (could that be me?)

My response to this is
he only needs earthbound eyes
to forget the children
that sucks him dry,
and ditch dreams
that pours out a telephone.

End of a perfect day places distance
between Roger, and me,
the wild-eyed woman
he certifies as bad company.

Merging sorrow cannot be shared.
The how of why people give life
to what they hate moves air.

I've come to accept life
in seasons of paradox.
Sometimes it's easier
just to sit outside and dream.
The day is compliant, and the
cow ants are curious about my toes.
I whistle and coo, and the birds edge
closer. The woodpeckers knock
blue ink swelling in my veins.
Maybe, I should just sleep all day.

The first time I saw a black squirrel
I took shallow breaths in numb surprise.

It paused in my peripheral vision,
turned twice before deciding I was
a threat.
I'm thinking did a skunk and a squirrel mate?

The sun watches me – caught
in a webbed day covered in silk.
Fog passes over my sleeping field.

The grass in late summer spreads,
smells new after its first cut.
The stiff fragrance stirs new ground,
speeds breath, makes me tail-jerky,
like a laughing dog.

Maybe, I was a skunk or a squirrel
in my past life. Gee-whiz.
I should be grateful for this life,
Though, it might be gone tomorrow,
I want more. Call me greedy.

Falling asleep hovers me above trees,
big pines and twisted oaks,
likes of which do not exit on my plot.
In my dream skunks and squirrels line up
humpbacked, move among the forest,
stagger and soar through dim air.
One turned, however, before they all left,
and in this filmy hedge there passed a look,
a concord, a long and measureless pause
that left me, on waking, with a sensation
of intense sorrow.

Naptime nears, and taproots thrust me
backward, drinking up the imagery.
I'm a tree in love with other trees,
a changing sound landscape.
Here pine needles thunder when falling

to the forest floor. Millions of brown
tips stand at salute.

All about me I watch the pines toss cones,
bend their heads. They are passionate,
as a woman anchored in lust,
calm in one instant,
full-throated the next.

A fence separates us.
My eyes follow the skyline,
and see black squirrels moving.
Smooth, marvelously dumb,
and muse-like, they wobble,
and sweep the faint air.

The fence line always stops me,
ways to keep obstacles in place,
defined characteristics of forbidden.
My C-Pap allows me to breathe
in the silence.

I'm told I'm a bush snowing in summer,
that I fall apart at the slightest hint
of rain. My Mother tells me I'm a Coleus,
one that always looks better when watered.

My ex-husbands lay claim
that I did mean things
to all the Toms I loved,
but I think I'm a Venus Fly Trap,
without food for feast.

My children tell me I'm a Four O'clock,
a late bloomer who didn't get time to grow.

I wish I were a wild day
or a thunderstorm,

through which you walk cool
with animal grace.

Lost tracks of time
and hypodermic combat with seduced spirits
speed the tightropes reach for stars.

The atmosphere dominates us.
Spells are cast behind Satan's door,
lightshows of secret societies wage demonic wars
and celestial invasions.

President Bush addresses the nation,
while we the exiled opiate sickness
over death in other nations
that whirl revelations
that rises up out of poisoned cities.

Mountains of tortured bodies is a revolution that
comes,
and tribes gather seeking oracles in my ancestral
mind.
Not astronauts, but Indians are the connector,
But we get an astronauts life whether we want it or
not,
leave behind one world for another.
Bolos of light unlock the TV mystery.
That's just the deal, like it or not.

Treasure's still hidden at the heart of creation.
Shaman synchronizer rewinds,
Tibetan projector illuminates petroglyphic
prophecies,
promises return to the Holy Land.
This address has the earth falling
into a trance of sanctification.
Fields grow with grace of new beginnings,
and enlightened we walk in benediction.

Gloom gathers beneath the tall pines,
crowds the roadside.
Past headlights families of deer stand on edge,
their eyes albino in the dark,
watch our passing with a mixture of fear
and alien curiosity. Asphalt turns gravel,
raises luminescent clouds of oily smoke.
A toilet bowl lays in the weeds, filled with flowers.
Can it be a lover's lane?

We park next to an ancient barn with wild stalks
of Indian corn reaching for the sky through a tin tear.
We walk a crooked hall on a tilted floor.
We are members of an orchestra filed onto a stage
against a bland blue backdrop.
Our strings surge into dramatic blasts.

Tonight's clear, cloudless,
sky-filled stars dangle in limitless depth.
At any moment my feet will hover ground
and never come back down.

It is in this instant
I realize life can be as insubstantial
as the shifty moon rays.
I squint into the harsh light
confused that reality has dawned.
I grew up in a Norman Rockwell world,
never giving thought to mud bogging,
good old boy stuff like flying
power-driven rides,
bouncing over rocks, spinning out,
sliding through potholes, gravel,
nettling angles, skimming uphill,
standing on the pegs,
hanging on full throttle.

A ride through open wheat grass
shoves me fast forward
to the wild side,
jumping half-baked boulders,
huffing in all directions.

Fast traveling together
through the woods,
trees flashing past,
branches overhead.
Out into open fields
of wildflowers,
the blue, clouds, sun.
Rain and mud,
deep puddles with feet up
for the splash.
Doing wheelies jumping out
of a closed down tunnel into mid air,
then dirt bogging down fast, staying tight
with my man in tow.

Never mind,
we both scale the edge,
power on.
Back to town, soaked and scorched,
machine thick with mud.
We're just pieces of ragweed and daisy flower
caught between the spokes.

Roger takes off on a wild ride,
as sunlight flips toward water,
evaporates, pours strange magic
of sand dives burning rubber.

At low speeds I'm flighty songbird,
complex, along for the ride type,

yet, entrancing,
minefield of ecstasy,
lying low mixes stone cold grief;
the thirty odd numbered child
still lives at home.
We should've cut the umbilical cord,
cause, I'm still flying,
estro-generation propelled,
full-throttled in vanity.

The two of us are driving proud,
poor, gentle people who struggle
in a real world.

Sunlight rises behind us,
fills the rearview mirror with blinds of light.
It feels good to squeeze the speed,
feel the car rush west,
chase the long thin line
of precipitous outlines.

Our souls glow like pink pearls pulled
from the bottom of the ocean.

We preserve antiquated traditions
of family, trust, peace and generosity
against the multiple threats
of armed cocaine-heroin gangs,
rapacious real-estate racketeers,
bad schools and brutish officials.

Roger's relatives drank,
beat him early in morning hours.
His father ran off after he was born,
rumor has it,
with an addictive personality
from Atlanta.

When he came home
he'd snatched a new wife.

After two Roger felt stuck, because
the color of his skin can't be peeled.

A way he deals with obsessive compulsion
I'm always loosing to.
He claims everything's okay,
Only, when he misses medication.
Our trip started peaceful,
but in rearview the mirror begged broke
backyard glances, each one bebop ping
to heat rhythms, browning pines,
each one contagious, squeezing sap.
This light squints our eyes
like sweet tarts, and mine are fixed
on him, daring him to match me.

An elfin's existence sprees
after prayer service,
it must be the way lovers ride
on rainbows of think tanks.
It sure beats the hell out
of staying home.

Little last tatted traces stain downhill light:
But, peaks have kept this view out of sight.
Views beyond them was beyond us both,
we saw no further than the next nighttime.
Grazing land would be there as surely,
as was the quarries which we couldn't see.

Yes, it's hard to stand still in canonical time,
rigid as a tent stake, hear the horses
whine in darker pasture,
smell the manure.

Paralyzed by the secrecy
of how a ragged cliff can bear
to be softer than the skin of being
that inhabits our world;
the late summer delights.
Apples, grapes, pickled cukes
are all sugary.

I love my accent. In it I'm myself,
nothing more than a girl,
mountain bred.
Chasing snakes look sideways
as if to say running is better.
Not able to compare,
this racing is what makes me climb
the fodder, the pains, the stones.
Suffering breaks sliver in fields
where I'm the lacking weed.

This is at all times my state.
Wherever I am, I'm what is missing.
A bare althea divided colorful, moving
variegated beauty where it isn't possible.
I inspect such contentment with impunity.
Surroundings brand culture on every strand
of nature and then leave me to ice over shivering.
Rivers run without arousal of suffocation;
freefalling waterfalls for mind's squat
in hiding mumbling mostly to fools
who have no wisdom.

The crow caws the fog away in needed time,
as field's intense stone rise up to our bends.
Sandy earth gleans over pans of muddy hands.
Straw strapped marks burn garnet,
angle against vesper beams,
and softly begin to glow

with town behind sheltered flume line;
panned view is a laid-back fire.

Grandchildren chase fireflies,
quiet their shouting,
as the shrinking territory slides
above short-legged.
Cow ants warp the views,
appear as speeding spots
at pasture gate.

Suppertime's arrived,
and tin ware's placed about
a newly checkered oilcloth
that holds double-lipped tumblers.

Rolling about shoots scripts
on left-handed sides.
The county fair comes to mind
since flowers pose for us.

One grandson whistles the hogs to slop,
propels dented milk pail,
weed-filled, over trough.
This is the moment we elect
to forget ourselves.

We watch wild chickens peck insects,
wait out pauses for pot-bellied
as they dine on greens.
Down the road a woman
named Vinnie always sits slowly;
a grouse perched on her guardrail
keeps watch for dinner.

Sleeping possums will soon poke out
to dine on dark car-filled roads.

Here we might choose
to live always, here where nasty rumors
of ourselves do not reach us.

In the whispered flight of kerosene lamps
the yawning truth lies open,
like a turned-down bed.

Land is dotted with cow ants,
sights of muscadine-hung-hiding-places,
and snakes curl in commas.
Not for a second do I regret being a hermit,
drowsy in a landscape
of vulgar black and white.

But then, there is the moment
when a splash of red arrests me,
transforms to spring,
summersaults intimacy.

Bright stars emerge,
vivid whiteness against navy sky,
pictures that revel old folklore,
and outline a chariot race.

Tuned piano music gallops
the heavy splay of paint.
Incandescence moves sphere
in epicurean sprawl.
Everything enchants me.
The night swells and quivers
on last notes, and we fall
like moths against the heated light.
I sigh to a magical moon.

Dreams flash on and off,
like myriad lights,
pale or rouged cheeks,
tired, yet sustained

by weary excitement.
I'd marry the stars tonight.

The dawn strips,
flings its will,
beats me to a new day.
Shoulders slump in sandy contempt.

Piano music crosses ground,
breaks the pane,
adorns my thongs,
slingshots me into function.

I'm a thin girl worn out
from giving birth
to a woman
on whose silky lingua sprouts flora.

My stroll past whispers is in a handmade linen dress,
tatted for shadows that weep with madness,
like when I was exposed to father's cancer.
I wanted to search his body for telltale spots
that corrupted my world.

That day the water bucket circled gagging eyes.
Dipper fell in slow motion, bucket into well,
dark shades covered eyes blue as glaciers,
falling too.

Black squirrels soared grass's edge,
combed back by wind.
Sandy earth erupted craters, curved
thick-mouthed warblers to sing sad songs.
Church bells now forever chime in patched sky.

No other signs were given and time passed
before Father departed and flew away.
Newly transformed in sparse light,

Gasps breath new universe,
gaze at the thin girl turning deals
with the flipside of death.

If my father were still alive,
he'd tell me not even a billy goat
could live here. It's like nothing
I've ever known.

He outlived his years among the hills
of Appalachia, a land shaped
by bulldozers, dynamite and
other hands. What I see now
is of our own making.

Night returns without notice
dazzling arms linger light.
Butterflies shimmer soft blue
scatter wide gentle ways;
wild beauty sings perfumed song.

Chords bond in infinite hoops
to early summer morning,
in plastered homes that reflect
shining seas of timber stir.

Pleated skirts conjure swift flight,
as sandy remains recover.
Pollen-crusted tangles hold
Grandfather's mustache that spring
not knowing what to look for.

Light in the dark disappears
into smallest crevices,
where beings crawl straight paths,
wait for minute spaces
to open up; poverty
escapes inches on edges.

When all else fails, there's Friday,
to drive me mad. Day slow dances.
Being a sister to the sun,
I am more desperate,
to feel his energy turn warmer.
South of border town breaks thin.

My husband looks for familiar signs:
The bathroom toilet with all its rings,
the wall where telephone sounds applause,
the humping hounds howl for more food,
then unobserved he looks around me.

For a little while, the sky clears blue,
and pollen falls yellow mixed in mist.
Flakes cover his flannel, burns my eyes.
I stroke shaving remnants from his hair,
but no one is there to notice that.
Kneeled beside aquarium, I watch.
Goldfish reflect me in their eyes.

One rosined mind snakes thin
strips braiding beauty,
threads copper on brown
glides side to side.
Pine needles flank path
by blackberry bushes,
and muscadine vines grow tangled.

Fresh feelings revive slow, rinse in sun.
Light makes every needled blade stand,
separates barks from tree with woodpeckers.
Their heart thrum knocks steady and insistent,
as my heart. How thin I think the membrane is,
sandwiched between despair and joy.

The morning shivers,
and I put clothes on
sooner than planned.
Old-time wish fawns,
tin tubs to bathe in again,
at least until spring.

Water runs brown from little gnome's night.
Their need was to run wild with dogs,
in this early fall. First month
where hog kills arrest me,
thrives where attention hops
atop a doghouse, howls,
under full moon madness.

It's Saturday and the flea market's packed.
Concrete walks echo chitchat
and the steady stream of smiles
overlap peripheral vision.

The maze of tables and luster expose
mixed sandpaper texture
of shingled slats baked rubbery
by the sun moves a distant razz
of musing, and leaves me blissful
with wonderment.

Sliced eons suspend trains
filled with thought,
one constant flow
of time marked by arrival
leaves before me a roused poet.

I lie between blooms,
and pens immortal verse,
rainbow toned,
where bobwhites dip and duck,
to sing about the cosmos in one flower.

Inebriated scents lure me close,
genuflected to one purple miracle
found on poverty's ground.
To sample one, then another
states how sweet the grape vine.

Muscadine suits earthly performers,
oncoming years drink rinses
in rushes of sunlight.

Every needle knotty pine halts tall
to rupture bushes in resinous forests.
Cardinals set off strummed –
tune-steady and happy hearts skip
braided beauty.
Film lies thin between despair and joy.
Greens and browns herald ocher-gold,
a biker's ride helmets calmer pastures,
cycles conversation, unknowingly cloned
in rhapsody of blue heart wavers,
signals tune keys for a madrigal.

Today there's a feeling.
Cluttered kitchen holds each last bud,
and drop of sand that is swept over.
I've been told I'd rue the loss
of noise in time.
I chase ladybugs out.
Hopes are they move on to another victim;
vigor must come to fight menaces.

We exist the best we can with yesterday.
Hysteria noiselessly descends,
like the beetles,
that seems to be always balanced.
Image of each day is forever,
fresh and grows
to the rise and fly teetering.

The green leaves giddy as me, until,
I become a tinted butterfly,
armed eyes long to be a forever fool.

Drawn back into waking world,
dirty dishes, laundry, and hunger want
to escape beyond the stained glass.

Clutter catches yellow sun,
and crystal winks. I shut eyes
to my heart, dwell, drift,
one curled pout lays beyond smirch.
I'm the slattern in this heart-felt line.

A smile edges, recalls hugs before fog.
Endless mirrors needle knots crossing.
Cold muller feeds on lunar speculations,
rests state of affairs until night,
and teeters slow strut
to stand still back and forth
with the grandchildren's thunder.

Cryptic instants drag face down.
Felt weight on breast feels
the many feet against my skull.
Then in soft cryptic shades words release
to make convalescence bearable.
Now sitting on other privacy fences,
home's garbled graffiti is whitewashed.

Only steady sunlight leaps off tinted wings,
to bear fruited buds,
in an eye blink.
Focus shifts the weave of wind,
and words blind stitched.

Ghostlike tapestries hunch edge
of twilight. The full moon drenches
sky, pale and luminous,
weaves the night,
fornicates sand,
pulls gossamer threads in and out,
sings song with hints of sadness.

I love lazy beauty,
the wild moonlight,
and struggles of air.

It exhausts me
to losses of speech
in this breathless atmosphere.

Roger's a busy apparition,
glides in like a New Year babe
pulled up on a mop.

I can't decide whether
to follow his mind,
or watch him hurl boogers
to time.

The night spell descends,
pushes moon,
clustered stars fall in treetops.
I imagine cow ants dotting sky,
shadowy ghosts that haunt me.

Cool bathes my eyes,
and slows the flight of insanity.
Life seems so intangible,
a melancholy beauty cracks deep,
springs upward and spirals me
half invisible to early hours.

These silent stretches burn my mind,
run through hair and overawes the spirit.

I think of how few ripples
our stones can make.
Have I given enough?

At home when younger,
butterflies sunned cores beautiful
in cocoon sleep, I watched them walk
heavy grapevines, drift like ghosts,
in hanging lines, soft and sightless threads,
silk flosses cryptically climbed tapestry,
lingua-woven to the sun.

Today, I can't remember if the dog is fed;
if the bed's been made this month.
Time works wonders as saw blade wind
chisels new patterns from thin shrubs,
stained glass effects of flora:
painted Monarchs hum
vain against vein rubies,
my mind remains stolen,
panned by enameled beings.
Therefore, does gentleness design
everyone's rise in mankind?

Tumbling bloody tangles of daydreams
proffering lineage opens these eyes
to glimpse gemstone outline of home.
Multicolored wings waver calm cloudbursts,
sparkle sun we all slow down to stand still.

Immaterial as carnival glass,
hobnailed and spectral,
flea-bitten rain covers smooth soft weaves
of a web called time.

Relationship is hungry for my body,
but, virtues starve in one address,
for I am a shy brown sparrow,
suffering many presences,
screened on mouthpieces.
Jackets reveal pictures.
Designer girl lives.

Turns are made in rocking rooms.
The mouthpiece is a vain hope
some have to scope.

Roger's love reveals objects I imagine seeing,
while looking at inkblots;
silk butterflies he smashes conceal his palms,
his words. His words slash stars,
a lightning storm in full display.

He lives in jeweled world,
where emerald serpents thrive
on forked tongues,
where music did his talking,
where my eyes turn on the lights.

Roger's slippery,
he can work death into anything.
His sunshine is headache-bright,
often bothers my eyes.

I flutter around this mad sunflower,
drink up the fragment of his sun
dished out drinking in his radiance,
forgetting my own wings now broken
particles of air.

He tells me I fly like a thousand birds,
and my laugh is like the spray
of the ocean.

Roger hasn't been a man in so long,
and my belief is he can still be one.
Misfortune might open his door.

Set afternoon is now a dock,
where this world is a boat
rocking stillness.

Let me for one moment
stop being all noise and color.

Let me for one moment
change the climate of my heart,

soak up the half-light
of some solitary thing,

lean out from this sandy land
in silence, sink deep into fine folds

of my cloak, and be strewn
over banks of quiet passion.

Love is a secret wrath,
an icy and diabolic conceit.

His mission is one to kill me
by slow death.
His mind's busy plotting
against my heart.

It is a form of prayer
in the exploding fires
of the loving embrace,
not even the gods know
what is real.

One baby field rat watches
sleepy eyes open,
not knowing what else
to look at or for.

Food in the dark disappears
into smallest places,
where my soul crawls,
as minute spaces open up;
poverty's escape
inches on edge.
Lost intentions surface longing.
Cuckoo strikes 2:00 am.
Sleep just another means
to endless passing of words.
What day is it?

The little lamp on table
has a white dog for a base.
Painted people and animals
live in ornate frames.

We're fools in love
baptizing piled devotion;
Our existence is lemon-ricotta
pancakes topped with walnuts,
and old-fashioned maple syrup.

Is this what I should get
for a lifetime of love?

Everyone, it's almost fall.

The sunlight bears down intense,
as a revival evangelist,
who helps raise all hands
to Heaven,
before moving on
to other towns.

The sunshine is golden,
that is to repeat the feeling,
that lies down deep inside me,
like an unhurried lover
keeps the feeling kept longer.

Each tree has a hundred golden hands,
soon to blossom out around us.
I hold hands up. Place lips
against the buds of the mums,
and feel how they quiver their tips.

Escape into the sunshine!
A much simpler thing to do,
than lose face with life and burdens,
people tell me I'm born to bear
each morning through doubtful air.

My children have reached upward
for years to gather sweetness.
They are virtuous and passionate
thieves of the hidden sandy hills.
Everybody thinks they can see.
My limbs long to skim the pond,
like a butterfly crosses feet
of shallow water.

Sampled pauses can weep
light into the air, scent flutter
up the path,
so delicate to shun fancy,
like some young mother,
holding out hope
to find her lost child,
or the moon,
or both.

Even before scent reaches
butterflies beat their wings ever so lightly,
to follow the bees that blow apple buds;
and then forget what they wanted there,
too full of blossom and green light
to care dusk covers day,
and dew will hurry to the ground.

I gathered flowers last Friday
with poetic thought
held breastbone deep.
I placed them in a mason jar,
until the plain round lid turned black,
and I began to cry.

Poignancy rushes rapid
to time's camaraderie.
Its definition being a well runs
much deeper than roots,
and recall comes flying back forward;
forms of desire climb
in worlds echoed.

Mirrors teach simple words that run hidden,
like cleanse and drift and drown and drain.
Friendship begins with quenchless thirst
for the real name of the world we live in.

A teacher once told me, "You feel with your fingers,"
dismissing expressions of love and fear.
She was an absolute ruler
that wore large rings.

Now, years later
I understand how to feel.
Fingers flip feelings from plagued heart,
howled deep inside when rim turned black.
Today will cleanse the drift where I drown,
and drain; shove poetry out window's pane.

But, pain will stay because of what was said.
Squares bordered by ridges touch
late fall's tree, intersects
at right angles hitting
fault lines above my knee,
mounds that once melted
your fingers.

No one would take it as gospel,
if I described the sunset.
They would chime in
tired fusion fired my brain,
the deranged writer of things
that makes them fish,
like unversed youth
in a poet's pot.

I, the great cloud-watcher, state
South Carolina is a state that gives up
its sandy acquisition of beauty.
In the sky the wings of gulls fly overhead,
like straight arrows of my efforts.

Flowers grow wildly on slopes
red cindered, sand beached
atmosphere frozen,
where water pushes bodies
that has nowhere to go.

Sand dunes fly
deserts white-hot
ensconce everything,
even palm trees laugh,
and pity mobile objects,
subject's lifetimes wasted.

I, in this same place
carry on my shoulder
birds of mountain song,
while the vessels depart
from one sea to another.

Now back, my bristly view
seems glad to make me old,
even though azalea blossoms
from clouded marble.
I read another poet that keeps
saying that only God makes trees.

All these thoughts are younger
than a morning smile and I accept
one observation: Time is not green.
Outside the sun rolls up her rugs,
and night litters stars.

My heart is humming a tune,
I haven't heard in years,
and tears carry tides.
Guesses are my soul is starved

for miracles, while my say-so spills
secrets further out to sea.

The stars are not far apart,
but draw closer with years.
It seems everything sags,
and they speak as a child.
In the past the ocean spoke
with silence and remained
just between Roger and me.

His clothes are the shape
and shade of need,
and he could be taken
for someone quite
normal.

Twilight closes into a yawn of brilliance.
But on the stroll back to the house,
Roger pulls me into the mock orange,
and the silky lingua of leaves flutter,
and make my Dixieland eyes sparkle.
There won't be time for coming back
with deceit.

The waking was a trust
drawn out almost unbearable,
until nothing, not even love,
built our delight in living easier.

Here the wind blows from nowhere
to anywhere, across a transformed state
by salt into a vision of light.

The low tide is free flowing,
but the high tide makes me ask,
Lord, Is this how it feels
to burst out like a rose?

I like to learn the way of things.
How do big colorful thorns grow
on the long stems of red roses
that dance and sway,
please multitudes
of romantic bees
and even flights
of hummingbirds?

As bee and hummingbird plunge
their silky lingua deep inside
I wonder whether it will fit
or break apart pollinating
with nature's music that enters?

With my face I lift upward in wonder,
could this be a type of rape that fills my heart,
or is this how cupid enters carrying bowstrings
of love, and then, and then, and then
we begin to dance, to dance for love?

Is this how nature loves to fly
on rainbows and valentine wings
that sails beyond the dark as it were
a certainty this should be the way?

I owe something I may never repay.
Such impossible debts are accrued
all the time, and would never have any way
at all to even any balance, if we didn't fathom,
and want to grasp, that some law controls
reality.

Maybe it even helps lead us
far beyond the tally.
Simply look back at the truth
of the world, and all the people in it.

Remember all the dysfunctional personalities,
the broken people trying
to piece puzzles together?
Remains of lives that will never be whole,
or in unison again.

I've seen their dangerous skirmishes;
certain survival against opponents
conceives no boundaries,
and has no compassion.

Madness devours my energy
that once used to burn
with hard-working fury,
when hard life was lived.
Tyranny seizes the day,
makes each moment
sharper with clarity
of vision.

I'm a native to the Appalachia.
Mock orange trees are native
to the Osage Indians,
and is Idaho's state flower.
But, I live in the sand hills
of South Carolina.

Memories of mock orange trees
in Leesville surround me
short-lived,
like hummingbirds;
People warble out of tune
with each other here,
can't sing as they do there.

This tree is very fragrant,
flashy and flowery.
It remains large and very green.
Although, prefers regular watering.
(May be related to our moon shiners.)

So much like me this shrub is often used
on outer banks,
or lakes and ponds
to poise erosion,
or so it is said.

Safer than a normal insecticide,
the mock orange doesn't kill roaches
or kill cow ants, it confronts them,
uses its pure insect repellant abilities.

I think my husband gave me perfume
made from this mock orange tree.
One time for pest control.
The ash from the Mock Orange
makes amazing glaze.
Merely, place one of these on
or in a china clay piece,
and fire to cone ten.

It makes a sunburst of red,
gold and orange.
Makes me wonder
what it would do for makeup.
I bet Martha Stewart has too.

Mountain skies have more stars,
Mountain fields have more blooms,
Mountain trees have more life,
and my life had much more love.

When I dream alone at night,
I find more happiness there.
May God not let me pass on
without going back there.

The hour arrives when evening raises its wand
and light smolders, after half-light,
leaves these lonely eyes
to watch distant sunlight,
step down a western staircase;
well endowed sashaying with rounded hips
ardent and crimson-gold ruffled crinoline
that turns the world of men upside down.

This place struts over memories that blow belching
opening solid past into boiling winds.
Long climbs past bitter vetch and shady strata
arrive only to look back across this hilly gorge;
all-knowing data that reveals with a red shadow
and folds into pleats of conjured blood,
where one might invoke the honed hues
of one's former lovers.   I've no such past.

I've never been a beautiful woman,
and now drawn-out, whiskered silences shuffle
only, to force me out across hilly gorge,
and stand with timber, grapevine and hollow,
equally old as the rustled tail-feathers
of the first chicken I killed for dinner
that pranced its bold puppet dance for life.

While others vault into a grave of love,
I carry on my drawn-out and whining way
with Horus walking in forms that only I could see.
Daydreaming led me to follow him,
and yet, he only watched me, a step away.

I'd be a pupil if he would be my teacher,
I'd kiss the ground to turn time around,
while murdering and castrating all the evil
I would eat black dirt like Ezekiel ate dung.
Then snowflakes would fall to earth and everything
would turn from crimson to white.
Pure consciousness would shovel all our paths,
and my head would no longer be upside down.

Skeletons and time are melancholy violins
weeping in lust for love
that was a rejection in waiting.

I emerge early today
to see the dawn-tinted morning
take its first deep breath,
not when dawn just begins
to ride the long back of the skyline,
but later when the languorous fingers
of daybreak slowly stretch,
across the tousled sheet of mountains
to rouse its paramour
with an elusive touch.

The skyline awes and then comes
with rapid rich breath of alertness;
a desire of understanding,
that a new-sprung day is at hand.
It's that desire I pause for.

It has to do with the light
the way it abruptly puckers
into the valley through knotty pines
and first fondles tops of granite rock.

This is the instant when morning awakens
and takes its first deep breath.
It has to do with the light.

My prayer remains
that when I come to grips with life,
there will not be that much difference
in heaven from this sandy mound
I call home.

I chose, at least for the moment
to believe in thunder's reality.
This belief makes my heart rap.
I smell an odor warning of electrical storm.
My mouth goes cotton.

Slowly, I settle my rump
in the lawn chair, not a metal one,
watch until my eyes feel mist,
and I had no choice but to blink.
A mere twenty yards from me
lightning struck, lit the field.
The wind from behind me blew
more insistent. A filament
of flash struck my shadow.
I stayed on for a spell.

I'd never been a deliberate girl,
never would be;
but even I had sense
to know I was acting insensibly.
But, I knew of how,
from an astonishingly young age,
I'd find a town –
some beautiful and intriguing respite,
home to me, wild things – and marry it.

Even on bad days my heart flutters
at simple sights
of a certain tree or twisted creek.
The stubborn green
of knotty needles seem
to be a marvel of God.

In the last two years my love affair
with the sand has brought me questions.
How can I have come
to love the inanimate in human emotion?

Together we might see
some worn night migrant
dropping down
to feed before moving on,
or some day migrant,
having rested,
departing soon after dawn.

We are all tired.
We are all searching for beauty.
We are all drawn to
what happens in our world
before most sleeping wake.

Roger pledged he'd never inhabit land
he couldn't pee on in broad daylight
without worry over observers.
He wanted to live
where a meeting with a bobcat is never
commonplace, but always a possibility.

Our state also releases coyote into the wild.
Tourists wouldn't enjoy the thrill
of eye to eye contact,
but the beach is two hours from us.

Roger and I sought to meet
in a place early mornings haze,
uplifts white from blue-black water;
moment's ardent clouds meet,
as spring moves backwards.

The sandy brook's face travels
branch shade paths
of morning sun,
where only we'll linger,
two offset medians set bushes scent;
one spreads chalky air,
and the other blooms bridal breath passion.
Obsessed, we seek the arcane diva
whose song flows freely,
from weeping willows,
like abashed ecdysiast
sway in and out
spindly limbs.

We'd rather ramble trails,
cross landscape we own,
in hopes we might slide
across secrets it holds.

Until the day I die,
I'll remember our daily drives,
walks, each inch of joy
our eyes have witnessed here
in Leesville.
What vision will I leave?

Parachuted views cross tea-colored sassafras.
Sandy shoulders arch mounds in slate form,
hangs heavenly shower, sheets miasma.

Beyond the sandy road
from Leesville to Pelion
a dog day rain wrings
its silver fury,
hangs a sail of water.

The storm becomes a lightning glyph,
splits the Edmund Highway,
incises a car windshield with jagged light,
a silver bracelet set with opal fire,
Egyptian cotton sheets
that Gabriela Martinez has hung
with a weft cerulean thunder
at Charles Town,
a brown girl lifts her tips
shapes of the rain,
makes jags of lightning with a finger.
Here she dances, pauses starvation
to grow angel trumpets.

I'm a woman who plugs her yard.
We have turned into burglars
stealing grass from right of ways,
because seed won't sprout in this sand.
I only want to plant the grass
so I can pull the weeds.

We watch with our eyes and hearts,
as the stalks we will not cut spread.
My daughter's chickens and ducks steal too.
They fly up the fence,
over my bushes,
and feast on the blooming seeds.
It is at this time I think of wringing their necks,
and chicken and dumplings.
My smallest granddaughter sneaks,
visits, asks me what I've cooked.
I smile, tell her chicken and dumplings.

She smiles, I fill her bowl.
After she eats I ask if it was good,
and tell her
that her mother provided the meal,
how all I had to do
was have Roger catch the thief,
and wash the pot.

She leaves horrified,
her mouth swells in shapes of rings,
and her eyes are bug-eyed.
What will she tell her mother? Or papa?

Shamelessly,
the chicken and ducks do not freely roam
my land anymore. I sit in my chair,
and watch the grass grow more.

My granddaughter rides her pony,
and doesn't visit me anymore at suppertime.
I'm sure my manic daughter wonders about me.
I should have told Stela
the chicken was IGA's weekly special.

I've become a scarecrow of sorts.
How will these children understand boundaries,
if I do not set them without witness
of the grasping talk my thoughts offer?

Love flowers all creation; embryos.
Consequence creates sunshine inside,
grown slowly with nurtured kisses,
forever being ecstasy once held happens.
Wisdom too will leave something behind.

Daybreak's not for the faint-hearted,
an excitement, a brooding, ardent
in a timeless and somber way,
eminent, grandeur and displayed
like loud trumpets,
but unheard.

Daybreak's a pendulant sigh,
a specter, scandal, raw-boned thinness
shrouded in wooly satin.

Out of obscurity,
in wraps daybreak comes up
like a noise one does not hear,
wavers back and forth,
wordless.
Listen to your heart.

When birds call morning in quiet rouse,
the bed drifts over daily rainbows.

Arc toward dusk lead the other fowl
to hunger discreet lives.

A little further on than me
people travel long-gone
in manners
of unobtrusive guides.

Every warbled tone is silence,
spaced-out enough
to shape the seeker's epigram.

Brief are the sounds,
as if to scorn sustained flight
exposes own feathered flock.

Laid out forms
of each other's barren limbs listen,
both to same melody; noted nuances.

Win over of awakened senses take
to bows
of silent ovation
that disappears with life.

Pictures leave imprints forever
on tracked minds.
People need to listen more
in early morning hours.
Birdsong can set free
the valuable migration
from downhearted ways
to a send-off of melancholy.

Take a break and soar high.
Life's a noise on the wing
some never hear.

All day I sought my self,
but I'm not there,
reached to feel my chest
but grasped at air.

Thoughts become a crowded scene;
a world of people, places,
and things without definition
carve me perimeter free, clarity free.

Then something happened:

I rise and give to those who need
a soul to hurt and twist and bleed.

I carve from stone faces to wear
with all my days of dying here.
I reach my chest.
I grasp the air.
That should be me,
my life in here.

Where's my childhood friend
that holds the atrocity lived within?

And to an inner child
whispers lie that it's okay
I didn't find my self today.

Daylight sprinkles Roger sunbeam colored.

Cleverly, he captures spectral pleasure,
blooms, becomes sunflower gala
that bursts full,
in impregnated wait for only me.

As these spells quiet shadows
in the stillness
of my ordinary life
after sight of him in silhouette,
tied up memory moments,
scatter joy, sadness, even despair.

Candy-coated the nightfall,
a coal-black void
breathes jitterbug light,
uproots the treetops to
extend for simple raps.

A sheltered rooster hears
earshot stillness sing taps.
Moonlight slaps me, and

I lay in awe, feeling
the conundrum of a loved one
who's so careful and sweet
clucks as he tucks me,
away from reality, unharmed
under downy and tickcloth.

No, it's not my heart
that reaches out to him
but my soul.
For what part of me
but my soul can extend
to him with such soft fingers,
slowly draw on his immobile cheek,
and collect the spill
from his thin mouth?

It is his words that tear at me,
and wound me so that my soul is free
to ascend to his face.
He speaks so gently-
it is not his calm voice
but his words that rend me so.

There is flush behind my eyes,
and yet I breathe as easily as before.
No pulse beats as cool as mine-
yet I am stirred so!

Oh, let him but speak again,
and I will never want for something to love-
Yes, this is the time that I call love.

Words are the catalyst of truth,
touch that great divine state
with every breath,
and bring pieces of it to me.

My heart still beats,
as it was taught
by greater acts.
Passion paces and purrs
within my breast-
timeless it says-
and it is his voice.

The spark was already lit
since I first began to move,
and it breathes his words
in and out, then returns them
for the pleasure of others.
Here is life and him whom I love.
Dances perform behind those eyes,
they muddy the water-
until they brown.

But what are blue eyes
to a man who looks at the sky,
and sees the entirety?

What is fair complexion
to a man who looks at mud,
and sees heaven?

There is nothing that I've seen
that doesn't pale in his words-
there is nothing that I've thought
that does not grow under his shadow.

In me - the soul may love,
as well as the heart-
but what becomes of the body if they
love not the same?

We're two lovers that watch
new moon rise,
over fresh-poured asphalt.
September's liquid heat covers cracks;
layer reveals tempest season.

Red sand from South Carolina
pits clutch print of his fingers,
one part of him now always,
as much as I am.

Tar Heel gravel pocks Roger's flesh.
Damp mist calls rain
sends old ghosts up
from sewer-grates
to foggy shrouds.
Cherokee phantoms rise
to lick salty sky.

Fervent recharges fix clouds,
meet kisses on one hand,
takes my mind,
leads me down Charles Town,
where lone Indian comes at night
to drink and sleep with nonsense.

Wild violets flourish in fractures.
Roger, the southern one,
with Irish blood, talks of time,
plows brick rainbows stretch.

Somewhere in the cobble I've lost him.
Drunken moon revels surge,
blazes brilliant
in fool's sight.
Stars spark over twenty centuries;
chimneys smoke rises,
jars what's always been accepted.

Here, banging heart bides blue,
and he, Irish-root of red clay,
gulf salt, river washed edge
propels oarsman ship for tide-pull.

He sears the sky I try to touch.

Hurricane winds burst on stage;
riddled clamber crosses driftwood,
and the South Edisto greets us
with unconditional applause.

Grand emotions clasp surface,
as we gather our roles in this wild,
unrehearsed production.

Shifted air marks the short-lived,
then to now,
sand moves my toes
to scale the looming storm,
and his wisdom holds firm
against the gales to come.

Air stalls, silent as the red sand.
We gaze cross treetops,
in tangles, stretch awakes
the rage that trails
exhaustion from storms past.

Fury, my hurricane-heart restrains;
bowed head succumbs to inevitable,
passion beyond my control;
the violent storm front
washes over me.

His eye sits in solitude of seconds,
encased in time humans cannot grasp.
My eyes blow distant, and gazed,
unfocused, past the presence of him.

Layers of a tempest season, similar
to dust-coated spider webs
worn by old windowsills.
Bent shoulders press forward
the sun and moon, and his footsteps
echo parallel my hurricane-heart,
clock tick-tocks;
futility struggles for immortality;
the tempest season booms.

Femur earth turns out juraled rapture.
Cradled red-breasted crests applause
its birth, yellow ocher captures cornflower's
mackerel sky that laughs with mirth.
Myriads of time have come and gone.
Scenes born from sandy womb trip over
silence gives noisy world retreat,
rivals colors, and presses bold blooms.

Few eyes embrace short-lived sheen
to gaze past Fall's golden spun cobweb
of dreams.

Surely, da Vinci's sight suckled
verdant green leave's dance
to turn grin and beam.

This left fielded painter knew life
to be futile, yet time's palette
lost all color for morning's desire.
Hope reminds me October's back!

Colorfully brutal chores stay.
Indian hemp nudges field's fire,
slowly, turns stilled life,
remains matted.

Persian red intricately woven
year turns, pats damask stalk's design.
After looks older eyes remain
wide-open to slants; a Venetian blind,
multicolored and not so plain.

I belong to fleeced flocks.

Poked beneath second floor window,
a clean raspy sound,
my grandmother spins:

Her two treadle strokes turn
the strings of my parental stock
into a lovely little wheel
with elegant lines,
curved legs and spokes,
my mother spins:

Dreams with elegant angles,
could handle the men folks,
just like her cherished mom.
But, I've no spinning wheels
to follow women like them.

In reach of finger and thumb:
My gel ink pen turns,
and I spin soft, low twisted yarns
with silent motors and hand controls
that change your speed or direction.

I'm just a splat at the Y-crossroad of life,
loose foundation for one housed on river.
Rocky people think murder.
Inkwells embody old bones
honed faces hang.

Black and white's not stretched simple.

Stone soup disturbed by a spoon,
in ancient kitchen room,
left past the living spaces.
Sweat halts scheme
of weepy sights.
Why two can't break clean, the cracks
between earth and sky?

The moment insists on indigo,
an hourglass shape
undulated by contra-dance.
Blinding scenes that send most men shivering.
Uncontrollable hair fires red,
sexuality channels
to a break in the earth,
shakes far from tempered eyes
of the sun,
far from eyes
of mere mortal's reach.

My splintered heart slowly fires,
a jadestone quiver.
Loose memories shift light patinas
in colored spaces that jerk golden hips,
risks everything,
the abandon of known universe
to enter lucid dizzy dance.

Eyes float suspended air,
and there, inevitably, all destinies die,
a death-in-life experience,
a rebirth in ecstasy,
inexplicable passion
for the strange.

Gazes hover us sway rapid,
beyond terrestrial existence.
Auras enter the dance,
Slowly, at first muse mysteriously transforms,
as air itself shimmers those eyes.

Those eyes!

The winds upturned rejoice.
Smiles dance rainbow beats,
beside sun's prismatic color palette,
petal-filled and laughter-spun.

Stringed lines of birdsong link love,
while wispy knots skip in-flight.
Swingy, flirty hands flower design,
blend moments cicadas rebound.

Yet, I drift off to music sometimes.

December 1st. Monday. In the distance
flocks of thundering clouds assemble
like heavy nuns running to mass.
My husband knows the thing I love most
is to stare out our office panes during an outburst,
the windows raised, valances ballooning, circling
round my muse on the edge above the keyboard.

This is when he decides he wants to hang the bulbs
that have occupied our outhouse for eleven months.
We don't own a ladder, so he lugs the lighting
upstairs,
where he lifts himself, backward through the window,
head and shoulders out, legs in, wrapped tight -
almost around my waist.

I have to anchor him as he boosts UL listed wire
to last year's nails.

His armpits are damp, drips sweat,
and his Jell-O belly shakes as he leans out.
He's like a power repairman strapped up,
trusting his wife to hold on to him,
his beer and balls.

Everything's hanging,
his hands are prodding lines
of currency that jolts his happy song
of Jingle Bells.

From the street an observer might witness
the back of a big man's crack emerging
from a window and inside, a woman
clutched close to the sill and his lap -
a job no missionary would take.

Or one of my in-laws could walk in as usual,
unannounced, discovering us there, paled
at the sight of their relative and that woman
he married entangled in one of the hundred
and six positions of lust.

He's hollering for a swig of beer with his free hand,
and I'm thinking of what better way to go than this -
embraced in my husband's thighs, high above earth,

knowing how the gossips will whisper of how we
died;
making love drunk in that window, oblivious
to the obvious problems with that picture.

How odd this afternoon appears,
lost like runaways inhale things
from others for their dreams to stay longer.

Maybe, Roger and I can sit on backyard swing,
eat strawberries out back of the clay field,
dip them in better bowls of refined sugar.

We eat saintly memories that drift farther away,
disease bends our minds backward,
like schools of fish swim upstream.

I knew in my first childhood the fly patterns.
Brim leapt lean, showy with spectral bodies,
the difficult fall off a simple cane pole
to an angler of sophistication.

One by one, fish fly away like faces,
each a cast-off scale,
speckled color fades
from summer to fall trawl.

I gather words like wiggling worms,
dangle them before his eyes,
trying to reel him in with artificial lures;
more modern rod spin-casts.

Tricks turn on us, we all age,
season jolts electrically charged;
neurons no longer shock or click.

My cinder mind pulls up sequined carriage.
Coachmen become rats, glitter become leaves,

think pieces know everything and something
has left as dusk descends; dementia falls.

Veiny arms and finger joints twist,
turn top on bottle filled magic.
Pills that lift the corners
of focus from night to day,
delivers darkness to delight
from ungodly shadows.

Every night, I read,
with straightened trifocals,
reflect villains slain
by charmed saints.

Grandchildren chant,
"It would take more
than a piece of magic
to conquer me."

It is cold and the log shifts
in a fireplace, lighting old passion's fire.

The grandchild moves her lips to run,
but does not speak.
No longer rejected,
I stare,
hammer the bronze baby shoes,
see another child
I once knew before her,
thrown into the storm,
of a time
when there wasn't any magic pill.
Weepy madness trails view,
I try so hard to push away.
Now my trust relies on a doctor
in a glass tower.
A little like magic, don't you think?

How dizzy memories come at me,
with swollen breezes spitting worms;
peeled truth from unforgivable fruit.
Roger lied to me. I bit his tongue
that always snakes charm out
of orchards, and bark
off the old apple trees.

Howling like starved wolves
we committed noise.
Like some hyped hippy I gave
him five minutes on the vinyl couch,
because he stared at me in heat,
with the eyes of a boy in longing.

Roger smiled the balance of the week.
I've smiled all week in memories,
taking the same road in reverse gears.

Remembering back to when we met,
at the Five & Dime with suckers,
his fiery lime-green lips flagged me,
we traded Coke bottles for pennies,
aware of the weight
of empty pockets.

The government rapes for power, offers bail outs, but
I rape from raging desire, offer no bail out.
Two fools had choices made for them,
and he promised he would be back soon.

Tears spilt like warm rain cross my face,
the day we were forced to say good-bye.
He stayed in that hospital for ten days.

Standoff between black and white edges
erupted those days,
where I stood in one spot,
on one of the warmest days
of spring.

I stared bird's eye level
with a gourd looped empty,
all thoughts vegetate goggled.
The door unhinges, two lips wet,
attempt knock; upside down brain
widens my heart
writhing to touch his picket's edge.

Scattered vines cling prolific world;
leaves swirl, sweep emotion verdant.
Virgin flowers climb bright in wild scurry.
Centrifuge curls around lost climax,
rustle, and vortex brooding brings.

Assumption lilies wonder,
if he'd just dabble my soul one drop.
Unwillingly, smell falls to dirt mound.

Shadows watch stones hump pale,
as my mind gathers,
wildly, embrace the plaster
of my dream is to see you,
where your face will melt mine,
eye to eye, cross pollinating me,
not a black-eyed Susan.

Undersexed moments bloom.

I am but a wild oat flower,
and warnings come rapid,
as tender touch presses alarm,
one into state,

to hurry ticking of heart.

Angel trumpets call from the other side
to long-journeyed passion
in need of answers.
Hope lingers that you will ask questions
of how to love me,
like every day was the last one.

Faith socks mute shade.
I can't see his face;
I don't know who he is,
but I know his scent.

If he loves this secret garden more,
then, what am I,
when the hard-set door breaks?

Call me a single collector
of clouded thought;
The broody one from Pumpkin Town
hatches trout, and the dark one
on sandy ground hollers.

Morning's field of cirrus furrows soften
over my seedy pasture,
first hold still,
as I dump the past,
like a dirt bottom fish sculls upstream.
Clouds slither away scared
from the collection
of manifested thought

My first husband smoked dope,
and drove to his death,
in a dying corvair
on a drunk challenge,
to Paris, an island,

where beer was not guzzled.
The two girls he loved were both blonde,
His mom and me. Me, who wore mini skirts,
that met the thigh high,
stockings that stacked brick shit houses,
and his mom, a nurse strung out,
she was always along for the ride.

His mom was a collector of sorts; mainly men.
I recall her winks and how she was so cool,
always excused for wearing no underwear.
Back then I was skittish and she was easy,
but sugary as skimmed honey from fresh combs.

The day he died, the day he was hung over,
caged walls of Viet Nam, I wasn't there.
When the call came, I sought him out, alone,
angry as ever, Marine issue coiled tight.

Now I challenge him back.
Still trying to get high,
I promise him this:
We will live faster this time,
much farther gone,
with the rolled top back
rushing in fresh, clean air.

Hoe clawing clay ground,
vengeance dawned ruby,
claims sparrow's feather.
Breath heaves morning air.

Two hollowed old trees
wildly flame dance wind.
Eye muscles sizzle,
startled into light,
like new converts come,

or the damned leaving.

Bristly breath rises,
as feathers plummet,
where sun always peeks.

I pull them myself.
Freshly cut flowers
sink the verdant grass.

Stirred up hillbilly
tugs at memory,
redolence of past.
Long-forgotten air
quickly seizes me,
rushes from thicket.
Rabbits erupt hushed,
cloaked anonymity,
tumbles from my heart.
In this wait is life.

Something flourishes,
yet soon dies leaving
winter hungry.

My cupboard is empty
of dried beans, hog guts,
and visions fly down.

It seems cows struggle.
Hills climb to meet sky;
vengeance is accepted.

Beyond me grace lies.
And, I drop my head,
in prayer to learn,
to be more thankful,

for what will be strewn
yours, his way or mine.
Halfway through December,
memories come
of mother shivering
in her resting place,
ghostly as dad at rest,
grandparents,
first cousins,
first cousins once removed,
countless cousins,
I'd never meet,
Who'd joined in marriage
without consent
to theory of relativity.

My memory whirls across a floor
cleaned with linseed oil,
to kitchen table,
where sis had climbed the old pie cupboard
over bowls of snaps, okra, tomatoes,
passed-on plates, cups, and endless buckets,
that once held the moonshine in silver.
Respect separated the water pans and dipper.

We all tried to reach on tiptoe,
glimpse life to be seen,
nature shows.

Nothing, we ever saw came close
to that hair spinning out,
pale cotton candy color,
hands flying furious,
always hurried,
on hinged skinny legs,
like shadow puppets,
and a mind reader to boot.

Mom danced the devil out of dad,
stunning distraction, turning,
to scold and lift her head up,
toward the heavens, begging forgiveness
for beating goodness, and faith into us.

After hours of watching white lightning streak
with tunes, across those plank floors,
mother chased us with keen sight,
hickory broke the silent moments,
switched our backsides.

Hard wind swooshed and righted wrongdoers back
to bed. Ticked bedbugs lay in the dark
to listen for play once again.

Now, I stand quiet,
as eyefuls of Depression glass glistens,
and adorned china claims me cheek-painted
amberina and carnival colors
knowing joy had thrived here, giving
reasons why I missed hearing
the shindig of old rain raining.

The cellular rang in the blacked-out kitchen;
later than normal, later than tolerable.
Yet Roger came for me, one who knew my story:
"Your ex-best friend is on the line."

I'm awake now, slip into the proverbial nook,
under unlit beams, where I could stumble forward.
Pulling a one armed chair out fully before
accepting the call, saying hello?

It's 2:00 a.m., maybe. Her voice slices waves.
The current distance breaks the thaw.

Spontaneous expulsion of a single word is heard.
My eyes jump backwards to the past.
My best friend's legs pointing upward,
the way arrowheads do skinny at the top
rounding to half moons,
buried into untouchable grounds.
Or so I had believed.
My second husband.

A loss she laughs at,
and her hilled mounds
lay beneath his,
hips wrapped around a minute penis
of time, and my middle finger thrusted despair.

While I'd watched them I remembered,
and wondered at the physics of life
charging upward still.

Two scarred stones carved my innards.
New thoughts after midnight,
five years later,
her backstabbing sliced cinquefoils planted
in past life. What assault did she want to add
to injury? Just out of wrangling grasp she said,
"Happy Birthday."

I'm a skeletal lover to the sun,
more desperate than most
to suffer his rays.

Eyes flash,
fingers run,
through yellow hair.
A quick grin covers
his candid face.
I sit sewing threads
of my heart,

hoping they will not tear.
With winter in his face
he relives our life
snow clouds pull,
waters stream.

At noon his guitar strums
near sundown,
as drying leaves whiff the air.

Earthen flowers criss-cross
in patterns old snows shovel.
Sounds become magnolia's drip
or longleaf needle's drop
letting loose their leaving.

The sun brings in aged shadows
to play, as my smile widens along cracks.

A snowstorm in bloom lights up
his stroked eyes.

Fair weather warns dogwoods
to stand still,
while you come with the glow
of thousands of words.

Faint wildflowers run,
after my feet hover
green woods here,
just before we take on new days;
coming year, when whole world will awake,
starting chances take time
from sunlight's splendid white face.

Come; let us walk into the New Year
to rock infant softness

to our pained shoulders.

Eye squats peephole diorama
to fetal-position,
sprays blue views,
the onset of wonder.

Peak's blue trill rushes
toward noxious stimulus,
cold glinted trout feasts
ease sheer clouds.

Sun delicate moans cool breath's frost.

Walnut's deep stains paint fingernails
acrid orange as wild carrots root run gold.

Wild turkey bears prints of melded paroxysm,
sips of pungent branch, and tastes future deaths.
Sand quietly weighs feather's sleep; winds
eye level needles, marches mounds of snow.

Pincushion cloud signals interpretation
in what man and earth smokes;
jumbled codes convey landscapes
allow for essence of what? Tell me.

We can't relate in poetic form,
even though passion flows,
sly red or vibrant,
from these lips tingle,
such as mouth salivates,
and tastes an apple freshly picked,
washed in spring water
where I ate blueberries
until skin dyed blue.

For I too grow wild,

in these sand hills.

By rights we're just guests,
traces of life that's existed.
Poets want to shed their skins
like distinct nature leave traces.

And the New Year rings in bony limbs
hoeing sand-filled backyard.

Lending her mind to buds of frost,
she thrusts hyacinth bulbs here,
and there she plants yellow crocus.

You can see her take color,
power stems beneath this spindly weed;
a shade of spring waits erect.

Roger will brick seven rows plastered.
Four borders you won't notice
will shoot up this place
in three month's time.

Not much good to anyone,
Me, a lonely old woman that lives
down Charles Town Road,
but I love to make things grow.

Suddenly, blooms arrive,
like the first day of a new year,
nurse my untamed spirit,
and keep me abreast,
paint pictures for me
when spring arrives,
when each and every one
of the flowers come.

Willows bend scent me lavender,

squirrel away my muse's tale.

Dogwood bud blooms,
loom out like the gyro
in a gyroscope.

The habitual horizon chases round,
desires propel past places
to points unknown,
beyond superficial boundaries,
manifests grand limits
of a guess.

Confines outside the long window look,
upon a field of chopped soybeans
that holds dirt.

I have plowed earth down
with little mind; less luxury hurries
on highway's bowed life.

Force might splash reds, Cardinal
on the wing, a flash smiles
the hearth warms.

Tears form one suspended icicle
in arterial thoughts,
where my mind melts
lethargic trickles thaw.

I heard shots awhile back –
someone tried to stop the motions
of life, a small darling one hunts for,
but I am not ready to be mistaken
for bird in flight.

I take sole strolls,

if only the safety
of the walls go too.
You think, you think my thoughts,
but I'm not fit to think yours.

Will you miss me just once,
if I leave now smitten
with blind sights,
from the sun,
or just one day grasp the silence
that takes on a New Year's tone?

False day gives stars rest
in rubbed eyelids,
after I paced the length
of my house, stopped at bricks,
stared at cement space;
belief at last I'd figured it out.

The universe fades me.
Craziness for a nana second,
melds to reason of why I'd dream,
His death in red paint falls about me,
flesh-making moves, new colored skin,
clothes.

Cliques known came deliriously,
close to figuring everything out,
briefly sane woke up hideous facts,
crept between two snowballs
next to my house.

A house I'd been left was in the dream.
The door was blown open to my sight,
and eyes prevailed to sculpted ceiling.

I recognized that look on my face,

revelation to various facts,
that it might be gateways to heaven,
or maybe it just held back hell's gate.

My eyes fell to tracks, blackbirds near home,
pointed prints in fallen snow this morn.
A hundred needled stalks of cotton,
bushes downed by plow tractor's frazzle,
seedy fields fingered two immigrants.
Crosses sandwiched topics and focus
yellows skin, yellows day, and yells peace.
Even though I'd never been beautiful,
my friends are well-known, right moves,
clothes and cliques.

I'd made New Year resolutions,
ran backwards in hopes of not falling,
frontward rattles placed slowly coiled
counter wise, almost snaking the dread.

My hair braided dark chestnut shades.
I offered my mess to peace,
then flashed sirens catapulted
past my stance. Red mixes blue lights.

Parody past my views spread out,
newfound wings flew toward end.
And enviously, my crystal eyes come
to mind how they must glitter gold,
decadent colors not so mute.
Insight or nightmare?

I've read riots of bloom; yellow hues
wake latent buds, and made things new,
and doable while words remind me of date.

Encouragement smiles and pushes me

to take my time,
as sun hides then peers out,
cautions against burrows,
a quiet cocoon
that waits lonely for spring.

From sandy hills the sleighs fly,
weigh heavy with hoary notes
to bore our days.

So search out your heart,
and look at life,
as sometimes it seems
each day is snowy strife.

Many say the world is a sea,
and sand hill's glory waits for me.
In my boat arranged oceans blue
sea green land lover's will drifts free,
foreplay dreams stroke earth's scented air;
despair smells fresh overturned dirt,
a simple joy so sweet entails,
visions see cost birth has prevailed,
questions worth prices steep to pay.
Brave you must be to climb the hill,
barefooted dawn stalks valleys deep.

Earth's wonderment not lacking strength
reach out to fading star burns your hand,
just so you may view far-off fields;
morning glories stretch sodden vines.

Mirth's wine births strange quest in my boat
digging toenail deep grasping coats,
many-colored dreams splash the rocks.
Loveliness reflects pebbled streams;
dawn's new day warms sun's reflection.

Truth's deep abyss denuding me,
a mortal for what was and is
naked under my coat of dreams.
Content with each baby born day
dancing dewy in fields of thought,
my boat secure with worms of truth.
Tired I reach my destiny spent,
my strength's passion holds no first mate
to part sea of sand hill's glory,
just sight's story swims between Earths,
veiled valleys of Heaven and Hell.

Mountains majesty magnified,
sky clearly purged and deified,
Burning hand outreaches fading stars
Now dirt filled toenails thrust upright
writhing on my back crying life.

Burning eyes beheld weeping fields,
hostile hills, hemlock clamored strife.
My heart now deep in prayer rocks boat
sea moans push on, no backward glance,
I spoke in echoes forcing life.

Just climbing prayers, no sea for me,
sand hills sprouting sin-sweet life
overturned by the boat of flesh,
burning hand outstretch tearing stars,
a fisherman's crying wails failed,
net meshed between Heaven and Hell.

Lonely as me, rays arrive
on country road heated,
soil bleaches thoughts
about existing poor.

Trees shade houses leaned
to race alongside life sideways,
where landscape gathers tributary.

Often thoughts come
about how rarely I ever see,
country girls, eyes paled blue, golden hair,
peachy skin that used to work fields,
and wash clothes in creeks,
wearing only vanilla perfume,
and flour-sack tick cloth.

Now only say-so heard is wind.
Bound persistent the rhythm blends mood.
Is muted shade that plays plainly day's melancholy?

I moved on and left behind the house,
where mother lived out her days
teaching all her children
religious tunes sang up storms,
spooned out fragrance flowers,
and herbal plants bring back spring.
One day she stooped over spiral bound,
and we thought we heard trumpeting sounds
of angel's flutter.

Those days are gone winged with no return.
Loudly left are their good-byes ghostly
on country roads,
turned pathways,
where sunlight casts spell,
blurring sheltered pathways
where only spirits fly.

Rainbows without rain border apricot sky,
burst forth leaving perpetual day,
sprinkle blue dots; spring's lonely birdsong.
Mirth-filled rye grass sprouts

amidst barren sand, sprays ray
cornflower blue sunbeam
become pearled tear.

Unbridled a goldenrod changes world
overnight, patch-worked freckles lie down
cornfield green, Egyptian forests lie serene,
and appear in wait of approaches.

Winter's guise wisp angel breasted clouds.
Outstretched spirit grows stronger,
and hangs over higher,
Awesome hues await decorated pledge.

Flesh tints spring night,
appears paler as eyes focus,
Mars held orange imminent promise.

View no longer shines ray,
and moonlight sadness parks.
Fate boogies silent breeze.

Unfettered gloom sloe-colored
in sudden aftermath.
Dying heart seeks bliss from guise,
winter bloom roosts murdered
in trees that root sky.

Face to face facts mute open ears,
deaf words worship,
fire fly flits,
garden opens secret door.
Alabaster rabbits sprint away,
as grass beats path,
bends and nods head in agreement:
Life short-lived can be capable
of releasing grief.

It wasn't as if he acted
horror-struck or strange,
though mother told her mother once,
at least his heart was good,
moreso, than other men's.

We called him Uncle Tom,
and it seems he never focused:
He rambled wood.
Daisies, madly bloomed, took day,
shot it, while visions ran.

We unearth him snowballed.
It wasn't as if he didn't try
to share first his claims.

Sun shines only on his porch,
then the wood rocker,
before it, silence too, and cried.
We tried to ruin his world
buzzing like gnats, child's play.

There was magic left in our space.
It wasn't that he didn't want to trust:
He kept secrets. Things he touched groaned,
thus he stopped, and called us "wise little fireflies."
So we called him into spacious home turf narrowed.

Smiling, he held his mind, hid beside thorny bush,
as light gave him a push grass moved,
slowly, crept on agile toes under sheltered rose.
His mother stilled past the plain porch,
hinged doors called faintly out of sound;
varnished her voice.
We caught his snoopy eyes measure us,
and more, light danced behind wind,
then poured out beyond belief

a child's voice we heard.

His hair turned to fields,
his dancing toes divided,
both sides hoofed,
two hands became birds.

Shocked, we held tongues,
listened to hear what pitch he sang.
Where had this trouble-free man gone?
Shadowy grass stood alone,
while thought wrapped peach boughs.

Honeybees ignored laughing wails,
dogs humped rabidly,
and we turned up sinking stones,
but only found white sluggish worms,
where grasses laid dead for years.
Suddenly, lost and cold,
we knew home turf lay bare.

I longed to touch and hold our Tom.
Grandmother's secret child smiles
tame or wild and stoned light and air,
his double-jointed hands,
his face filled that bare place.

Slowly, leaves turn back to black hair,
birds waver into hands;
smiles madly blooming stop.
The starved man steps forth, stands stiff,
like one who knows pixies, phantoms and solitude.

On dewy grass, he walks nearby,
our limbs and snippy sun exits down,
all absent, but us.

Grandmother sang storms in the house,
kept dinner warm and loved us,

God only knows how, or why
earth remains so shadowy.
Leesville serves up a mosaic dish,
sandy poises cross-littered heaven,
glossy blue, it should be a capitol.

Green-tipped peaks maneuver
shadow to heart. The memories
chill. A Peanut Festival wants more.

Bright sightseers will be generous
to our town beyond belief.
Swiss-dotted tutus swirl cash,
sherry and gold marmalade.

Backwoods populace would settle
for less. Then they pray more often,
than when they're terrified,
like now, inside panes looking out.

Golden maple rises and chickens
roost; the richness is restored.
Intimate parasol's cover teach
walks near grace see beauty.

Seamed populace candid and close,
glassed butterflies pulse,
endure moments.
Whispers smile and whir quilts
obedient among the kept.

Secret birdsong chirps air.
I sing my own sonata.

In the morning read one stranger totes hint
of apple butter, quietly rustles red oaks.
Cimmerian soar overhead, a sentry single boxed.
The sun has risen in orange linen. Old mourning
returns again, and ears pitch Mozart.

Piano sonata's gentle, my smile sinks,
falls blue in the basic repertoire
of sunrise whimpers,
plays to tunes tawny owls hoot.

What is left is a mysterious tone.
Footprints drift in the garden below,
someone has left quickly.

How harsh this autumn is.
How serious season face shifts
Shasta that peals back
in sensual petals
to pick blooms.

Daydreams obscure the slumber of leaves.
The dark gold of rotted flowers face off,
surface brightly. Roger's eyelids heavy
with poppy dust and he softly dreams.

My mind tinkles and trembles cold muller,
much like four doubled strings
of the Guitarra Latina replaces Pyotr's
"Overture of The Seasons",
"The Hunt" and "Autumn's Song" draw closer.

Familiar step bends eyes upward
to jackdaws in flight,
a vision of black rafters,
an open window in which hopes fly.

Purple flame of my silky lingua leaps
mouthy into stillness, my soul's anxious,
and lonely string-music dies down.
Silently I lean over the edge,
study the blue face belief offers,

while that oak consumes red flames,
and fury flutters past your heavy eyelids.

Round the field firefly's light,
their bodies heavenly and dark.
Watch them fly over barbed wire,
like ghosts in hanging lines they dive
in spider webs, outfitted prisoners
captured in tapestry, silk-woven
to the moon.

Therefore, does disposition design,
our rise or fall from bloody skyline
to apparent junctures that fold
our eye's quest for redemption?

Imprisoned fireflies flicker soft rain,
sparks sun, in disembodied madness,
spectral bit, rains gaze forces
silk-like texture
of a woven web.
We haunt unsettled choices,
burn faith's door,
as he carries us into moonlight
calls all his fireflies
that flew in the field,
held by the web,
and hope they hear
his call.

A silence lives in the panes,
Sun doesn't shine for the end of summer,
cloudburst falls from the eaves of gutters,
wolf rats scurry here and there,
seek new sewers.

Softly, gray mist follows the insane squeak,
and I'm but a shadow far from paranoid city,
and drink in the silence of God.
Water spiders glide across my heart.

I see you strangle under the garbage,
left stardust blackens my wave;
metamorphose changes my whitewashed soul.

Your dreams turn dark
from crumbling walls of pain,
your unhurried voice soars,
deprives wordy ribbons
in dark waters of rained on spirit.

With birdsong and germs, here,
on Indian land seeds wing acres,
cross the unsolved mind.

Scattered zip subdues farewell,
addresses heritage,
alongside daybreak picks,
and greets a long drawn-out day
creeping river's way.

Toward the south gushes,
pass leafy involucrate thickets
where rabbits rush.

His guardian angel's heart climbs
to succumb once more.
It is the stubbly facial stares back
of lonely rain, a seething wind that rings
my bones.

I'm the bleached tree that stands alone.
How melancholy my day,

as I have not yet lost heart,
and live with anxious wait
for new beginnings.

Every day brings short deaths,
and we drink from life with handshakes.
Leaves drop; steel guitars play a vibration,
cemetery of life has been reborn.

Winding-sheet wrinkled willows pattern the south,
drafty dry, long-winded with never weeping gusts.
A black crow's eye stares down the ornamental man.
A wire pie pan around his breast,
spins cross air.

I run fingerprints down the glass
to savor the crystal pains
sown by one forlorn soul
and two faces.

The standing timber recants her reputation.
She wasn't always double-edged and warped.
Burdens built the hollow bough,
reasons most fruit bears flavorless.

Seven years and a month ago
one blueberry bore flesh of males,
long, and shaded.

Painfully I rumble this memory,
identical stains split
of red on crooked walls,
a spring I'd never known before.

The garden heaped bloom and faded,
twins born amid one deep-freeze.
Two bushes entangled, broke mixed,

and unyielding twigs fell between palms,
more heavenly than hands of dust.

Beyond the winding-sheet of wrinkled willows flap,
I couldn't cry and the black crow's eye hovers.
Two faces delivered
to the wintered world and me.

Instead of black crow's eyes,
two slow tan feathers float down.
Delicate bones, fingers with black hair,
and brown eyes hungered
to kiss fire and sorrow away.

A spring of everlastingness revives my soul,
and now a desire evades the mixed,
and unyielding twigs.

Often nights return to try and make me old.
So, with my twins why should I be lost,
and lulled to pray for a forlorn soul,
when she wasn't double-edged and warped
with burdens that build the hollow bough?

Juicy sparks from her mouth to my mouth drain
illusions from sky, self-deception, it offered:
pale clouds amble home the winter,
an autumn landscape where we lay bare,
dust blows exotic desert, so far beyond,
summer's fruit within ranges of love.

It is true I'm as twisted as the cactus,
that gnarls and turns neighboring swarthy,
light cuts fingering hearts easily knowing
nothing of cold hardy bleeds that pain,
and shoots near hand,
plus mind floats above stickled
yucca rostrata lays wait for love

to rebound on mushy melodies.

Drifts of white blossoms capture my breath,
and writhe like a stripper turns her backside up.

We lay and listen to the Gila monster sucking;
heated half-light sears water from the blossoms.
Seeds fall for hours in sunned trees of boughs,
while sand dissolves underneath jackrabbit's heels,
leaves echoed window closed, door open.

Some waterfalls slide and stumble fetching still.
The day scrambles empty hill.

Roger comes to cut me with a dessert knife,
as I, insanely, lurch against Joshua tree,
snatching white blossom that floats away,
Bough breaks, splits the skin, severely.

Out of bark range renders many footprints,
and my mind's fence swings wide open,
raw hinged toward cliff of love,
a cold curve of sand,
twisted cactus rose,
a limped penis thought,
and balls of stone.

Beneath soft feet's cries,
sadly, seared airs I hear,
as he hurries ground,
and slips into my arms.

My name reveres weeds from Hell.
Lonely to hold, his flesh drifts;
white blossoms walk
moments ride away.

Kit foxes' flute silver,
now thin and lost,
over and over.

I'll return some evening to discover,
this cactus raised to the very root.

Summer will be gone.

A reckless heart in me belongs to another;
so maybe you were robbed.

Eyelashes of morning can't blink
in this undersexed hour,
when universe remains redolent.
Human lust can be sad.

I'm sorry to have stolen your heart,
but this broken-hearted think-tank

formed from dust feels nothing
for creation awaits my fall from grace.

Pain dresses me like a woman in depravity.
You offer up roses, black in my mind,

meant to thaw-out pouting silence,
I walk away copulating other loves.

All the trellises of my garden mend old fires,
shakes of turpitude, so casually.

Screaming toenails pierced from fallen
honey locusts make me weep out of sight;

sore views from an old blind woman.
Look: I'm nothing.

My seed only grew into needled pines
of loneliness of which I'm drunk on today.

Lost between the Nag's head near Virginia,
and where bee boxes loom,

past dead chinaberry trees,
A reckless heart in me belongs to another.

I was so beautiful, and I was his snowfall
turned to a white charger standing still

beneath dark snowball bushes,
and now he's died a public death.

I claim the secret right to be ashamed.
There is no place left to go,
will Roger take me back?

Positioned depression compels me,
wraps green-strings
of waxy watermelon,
lifts muse propped on southern bed.
I traffic-clog a metal steed hard
to ride south, to see home,
where seeds are sowed,
and mistletoe.

Back then in Southern sun
our eyes elevated life's glitter
in daylight's fire.

We circled fields on Carolina weekends.
I've become a sharecropper
that collects strays.

Roger helps me pick better limbs
to swing from.

Then we fly toward the sky,
tire tubes high.

Cold feet flamed my chained hands.
He said I was brave.

I see his mother's face light up,
colorful rays burn the sun
I've come to see.
She's poised, hand resting
on tire tube's heated tar.

She smiles the way Sunday
taught me godliness.
But, one day he dug up his father's grave,
a country churchyard now cutoff
by asphalt road,
and didn't find the pine box.

Just an arrowhead,
we thought was petrified.
Roger took it home that day.

I remember that last long afternoon,
and his mother,
how we all looked,
as she shot herself,
bullet buried deep in her head,
but she planted this:
Nighttime dreams of seed and us.

Green watermelon harvest turns sleep
that holds us, and I still hold on,
I wake but Roger's gone.

A medium utters in my sleep,
"You see what is not there.
I will do a reading for you."

Life remains drunk on memories,
and needs arise to erase those comets
with their projectile's path migrating
furrow-bound toward this southern soil.

We used to play the hangman's game
of words. He'd guess to fill the blanks,
but his letters missed,
and I drew the hanging figure's arm or leg,
until bit-by-bit the body suspended.
That was the game I won.

His mother plants a slug in my brain,
bloom in summer dry rots the winter.

Every songs a love song,
a light in the sand hills
where bone dust fluoresces
into fearful bloom,
and red birds sing warbled blues.

Slutty blossom shift shrugs,
apparent magnitude,
and diaphanous clouds
court unsullied sun,
but not in hot pursuit,
more coyly, here in Carolina.

Black squirrels flicker the magnolias,
one by one, like criminals they angle
manna feasts, fetched ideals
that feed on my brain.

A match strikes,
eyes ride-wet knuckles
of the longest limbs,
silver maples grade glissando,
over silky lingua of dogwoods.

The old hound bitch poises
one paw leveraged
out of the soggy grass,
then another blithe dog
has nothing to do with this:
too old, too slow.

Night-loving snakes lay
under yellow bell bushes;
curl clusters of commas;
the water spiders spin
silky swaddles of gauze,
in wait of quickening the hour.

There is no heaven on earth,
or simple choices for one responsible
with the care of so many others.

Like red birds that are able
to sing their warbled blues
to a hued horizon.

Where I am,
berries bear.

Where he walks,
a red-tailed hawk,
beyond death's rail,
dresses a feather, rests
to climb the limitless sun,

from the paleness of his breast,
taking with him tones of my heart,
dawn-tinted, beaten gold and baubles
before I pretended to be a thing of light,
whose whipped wings would never silence.
And indistinct domestics are all at their chores.

All around the South Edisto moves,
mocks slide of fish that jump,
and reveal them reluctantly,
such as insignificant beings do
when revealing their nature.

Changes of heart become separable,
and snip-snaps stand upright smoldered.
Apprehension for others appears gradually,
and disappears in years so slow that nothing is
different. I recall sunshine the blur of pale candles,
a small gold wedding ring, tall columns of light creep.

Not until his Mother died the river asked, "Did you not
know you can't live forever?"

Pecan season is almost here,
and I've walked
to the middle of the grove,
so I can see the places I'll pick.

Everything is sand and swamp,
and the fresh greenness
of a small town.

One day my children will leave here,
go somewhere they'll never pick pecans,
shell their fingers sore,
but stain their nails
with a different flavor,
and it will be like these moments
never existed.

Summer puffs warmly on my lips,
his revealing breath against my ear.
A home nestles in dogwood blooms.
Delicate rainfall balances new flora;
taps at pane with limited embrace.

Outside I come to sit on the porch
peer past gray southern clouds,
rainbow flings out yellow shade.

The towering vines of Charles Town,
and two birds stand guard
over their young
perched in tendril outlines.

A stone's throw away wet rock rolls over,
as black squirrel's limbs push fuzzy tails,
jump limb to limb, and birds soar in pairs.

Inside tree's branch young mouths open
to fresh flight that feeds worms.
In slow motion they chirp full,
and shrill bristles green grass.
While the birds watch the squirrels,
I watch the birds.

Someone once told me
brainwaves of birds match those
of insane people.

When the squirrel turns
to other squirrels,
the birds turn
toward them,
and angle in wait.

The birds watch,

make oblique darts
into the danger zone,
to mark ground for dear.

The squirrel is jumpy,
as a death row inmate.

He's a sociopath trying
to match the bird's brain.

One flashes teeth,
and bounces out,
like an insane person
in definition:

It now dawns on me
why my mood swings
back and forth with Roger.

Even when I'm naked
I'm fully clothed,
my body a landscape
of color and design.

We meet on street corners,
the sky pale purple,
the air crisp.
I inhale deeply;
the cold air assaults
my raw throat and I thank whomever
is listening for this moment.
He's handsome,
he's perfection,
he's my fragile angel.
I know priority I give him is undeserved,
but when I look at him,
I see only the mask of color.

He reflects light,
causes me to see only
what I want to see,
obscured from what is truly there.
I choose to ignore what I already know.

I can only think nice thoughts
when I look at him,
and sometimes when he kisses me
I truly believe the things he says,
I truly believe that I am the only thing
that he needs, I truly believe all of this.
Sometimes I believe in infinity.
This life's course is short,
half hidden by tendril green,
from source to stream,
small enough to detail life.

Hikes along its twisted flow
between honeysuckle scent,
birdsong and the bleached air;
pale rose sky in sun glimpses.

Steps tread splinters
of time, gasps breath
like day comes to life.

Rumor has it that one can contrive
geologic outlines of the mind
field, hill, river, and the thrill
of shallowness.

Illumination faced today causes climb
of life to turn challenged,
and panic stares back from puddly messes.

Feeling dies, becomes the red rose

under the winter's snow now cries
for spring's breath one more time.

This life yields to a new discovery.
There's a stranger that lives inside me.

Each time I wake,
a quiver or an eruption exists.
Something within me wants release,
and always it seems
I have just dreamed of death,
as all living eventually do.

A secret lies buried inside me.
I trace a finger over cleavage
of my chest, try to believe
his mind grows normal,
his love is for me.
Maybe, even in the way
saints come to love pain.

Lying awake at daybreak
I think I'm like a bird in 3D.
Astral travels fly out
of my skin, memorize
that looks down,
as my cleavage rose,
fell and pulse quicken.

Memory sounds
of pounding horse hooves
on my chest.

Startled awake
I trace beneath expanse
of space,
a blur wet with mist and wind.

Tears of amazement
watch violet heads
of daffodils erupt,
stiff from earth after dying
for an endless season.

I feel my white head appear this morning
after entrance from the next world
to come back to this one, dazed.
It is the way of natural query
in the present world
to understand this place.

My dream was of an arid room,
sun beats a younger woman
who plucks daisies,
throw them on his chest
with a flash of silver blade.

After all this heart breaking destruction
everything and nothing changed.
I'm still the animated mountain woman,
who found her voice,
who dreamed of having her body cut away
from him like an elegant rose.

This morning when the last star dims,
and daybreak shifts toward mid morning,
I realize it's been ten years,
since I died before
and was buried.

The first time in Mexico
where a language of love
could have freed him
from his stroke.

I heard about the affair in Mexico,
or maybe it was Texas.
How the wind howled,
and pulled everything down
in a righteous anger.

It was the woman in me,
and not the child
who explained real life,
and now I accept the insight
we have both arrived at
of the ripe meanings
of a living death,
and how life ten years later has slowed.

Changes of seasons
when we had just begun
to touch the whirlwind
of our life so crazed,
and artistically balanced.

This is the secret that is buried inside me.
Every day for ten years now
my wild mustang stares
at the oak bough outside
his window where a woodpecker
knocks the cry of Thief! Thief!

One night, I know the dream will end,
and I'll bury my fist deep in his chest,
and I'll tear out his living heart,
and raise it toward the man
I first loved,
and whose soul I can't recall,
and I'll shout out,
wail a long cry
with my final breath

that will fallow with fugues,
Take it back! It's not my dream!

One pause beyond the dusty dew
an abundant tree nymph rises,
early in daybreak
to muse around the treetops:
Momentary images reach hands up for prayers
to soften severed significance clear, one voice
storm-tosses their meanings well advanced.

One sound beneath roaring elegies to birdsong
call complex whistles to cold waters creek crawl.
Obsessive tangles twist the cast of characters,
and unturned rocks lay out daybreak thoughts.

Bare soles feel fear that unfolds paths,
and seeks out change of clearer recalls.
New places meet with subtle insight safely kept.
One ponders when the commingled briars,
blackberries with thought will cease and die.
Snake venom tooth marks words sliver:
Birds of prey fall into tailspins
of the ferment.

Their bodies submerge in streams.
Lost tree nymph's image declines
to nothingness; but, high puffs pull
one simple cardinal,
a speck's drop from heaven
for the red eye,
and, for the ear,
under the muse of snarl,
gropes summer,
and winter's words have grown old.

One solitary human hums words

for love of life to sort the tangled strife.
Openly, the cardinal soars,
and summons the rare hunger
to thrive and rise strong.

Sprays send me careful rules of song,
a miracle out of gray sounds,
rise as the moon fades,
and dunk damp birds of prey.

Swell forms the informal sky.
Woman or bird, I plummet
under pale sounds,
parade away
from the nothingness
by the rules now made:
Live for light,
and let the silver measures
die before voice dies.

My words to him are unfinished,
where they lie common and naked,
as mica stone in granite veins.

The forest still moves,
and the world slowly subsides,
lapses like the birds of prey
fall into tailspins.

In a mindless dance,
beneath the snarl,
I send Roger creeks
that echo of my voice:

Let the leaves whisper in his ear,
and the sunlight kisses his face
while the water runs over his soles,
as fear unfolds paths
toward the moonlight
that shimmers from my eyes
that remembers.

What sapphire of ocean or heaven
has deranged you?
Sea nymph of land that solicits
intensity and forever falls pallid,
cerulean not turquoise,
always falls peculiar
to the true blues.

Iris and delphinium
grow well-nigh to his shadow,
making scorn of him.

But when the blues fade I remain:
fine thorns, bony lace,
complete, eternal,
as his yearned silence
to live out all my poems,
and run with ease
for the love my pen writes.

Foreseeing my eyes smile,
sends shiver my love.

Trailing beauty grasps
no bounds
to the rhythm
of my heartbeat,
forever real,
loving him,

sea nymph of land.

The air's too cold tonight,
observe the trees.
Those hot dressed Mexican women
he saw picking beer bottles out
of the street today
could have been a warning
of some kind.

We press our faces against the window,
Watch foggily, as one blows oxygen
into a crushed can,
in hopes it would expand back
to its normal shape.

It proved precision
of my attention to detail
with almost irremediable scrutiny
to watch beauty poise in such squalor.

I abandon the outcome up to you.

Motionless in the face
of the frozen food case,
I see Popsicle's
and remember
the way Roger sucked
the breath out of my body
with steamy kisses,
and remember the first time
outside the drug store
he wore bell-bottom jeans
and a flower power shirt
stretched over bulging biceps,
and I in white peddle pushers,
legs already suntanned.

I licked my Popsicle hard
to keep the sweet juice
from dripping down my chin.
He held a boom box
on his shoulder.
Up, up, and away
in some fifth dimension
his fried eyes
and brown lashes
brushed cherry cheeks.
While his looks slid
down my bones
(I an innocent 16-year-old)
tossed my stringy hair
drifted downtown
fully aware, he'd follow.

These winter hills of older age
turned stars on last night,
and thoughts revolved about love.

Dreams started,
of all the darlings,
of the seasons,
that I'd known,
that wrote me love letters,
gave me diamonds,
decorated me in furs.

Yet, I allowed them to climb
their own trees,
and let them take nothing.

Now I wonder if the price for my escape
from their offers of freedom
should bring pity for myself
for not taking more chances?
Yellow bells sprout on the hillside

of 2007. March winds
and no rain for days, the silky lingua
of the red crabapple struggle with morning prayers,
tulip trees and sweet gum seek out forgiveness
by the dogwood blooms that spread budding gospel
down Charles Town's way.

Morning reissues its warning
middle age rebirth is work
and not easy work either.
You now know why I've come.
Sunday's best flowers and dinner spreads
leaves me to wander why sap oozes,
and a lonely soul debates serenity
over a stone-carver's latest pride;
begotten passion taken from me.

It seems everything goes through it:
The sun's rise each morning,
The mockingbird's flutter,
The rooster breaking sleep's hush,
Holy rollers reeling out in rapture
every Sunday over and over in my mind.

The magic starts and I know
you, my angel, weep in ecstasy
to hear my hillbilly alleluias,
and lay in wait for footsteps
of a lover that lives to meet you
and eat sour apples and weep
for the end of this season's rain.

June is mysterious,
and diamond dusted lilies bloom
of speckled light, the rising night, rings
of stars, stars, that slowly fills the air

But what of the ones who lost the stars,
there is very little else?
No stars, no love to paint the sky.
Love's throb evaporates to air.

Of all the sounds that are left, little is left,
for men who shift the shadows of love,
by the shades of their eyes,
and the tones of their voice;
they need not fly, as women do
for the sky, being theirs is conquered.

Circles through my heart change daily,
and leaves June with curving winks
of contemplated fireflies in the dark,
and deep in night's speckled light,
the falling stars no longer sing.

I rose early today
to see the dawn-tinted morning
take its first deep breath,
not when dawn just begins
to ride the long back of the skyline,
but later when the languorous fingers
of daybreak slowly stretch
across the tousled sheet of mountains
to rouse its paramour
with an elusive touch.

The skyline awes and then comes
with rapid rich breath of alertness;
a desire of understanding,
that a new-sprung day is at hand.

It's that desire I pause for.

It has to do with the light
the way it abruptly puckers

into the valley through the knotty pines
and first fondles the tops of granite rock.

This is the instant when morning awakens,
and takes its first deep breath.

It has to do with the light.

"Never fall in love with a poet," I told him.
He gazed so lovingly at me,
and then the needle-knotty trees,
while November left on hashish colored drifts.
Rhymed couplets gently roll off sleeves
of my flannel shirt.

When I closed my eyes, and recited so clearly,
my voice cracked at the depressed lines.
His chest still jars at the wink of her eyes,
and he should have listened,
and never fallen in love.

"Poets can break a man's heart," I softly spoke,
in swift shakes of my head.

Then I pulled him closer
into my Carlos Williams mood swing
of meter, lay his arms around me,
rocked back and forth,
to the beat of my soul,
freely versed thoughts
directed his ear.

Freedom thundered,
and Sunday spirits flew,
and we sank to our breath,
where everything dies,
and everything is born.

Cycles incomplete,
circles complete.
It's my fault,
his fault,
but all is perfect.

I'm the sunshine on his birthday,
the stomachache he gets from eating candy.
He's my last cigarette break,
becomes a pesky pet kitten
that feigns sleep
on my lap.

Our scenery changes and melts,
while I hold him on my tongue,
like a whispered rumor
that runs fast,
and explodes.

Then we wither
around my words.
"Never fall in love with a poet."
These things only happen on poetry days.

Lunar Phases

Cinnamon sockets drink coolness;

stepping madness rings darkness;

rushing from rocky blue springs.

cowardly full moon revolves bed,

Pretense ponders mysteriously,

fevered sheets sweat out night.

crimson stillness pouts mouth,while evening looms.

Intensity as ambiance remains solemn.

ends absorbing lonely ghosts

Leafless undergrowth shoots

in secluded stringing prayer,

Face hangs double-edged.

Psychosis devours the sane.

Somewhere kindred birds much wittier survive.
Few tarry to shiver in the storm alive,
smart ones fly south.

Meanwhile, many faces dart the wintry stage.
Subterfuge is lost and fallen in snow.

Hardly any bathe to rinse in tinseled blow,
wilted pinwheels petal bough on cellar's hill,
lonely for half-hearted days that left with will.

Limbs flap, back and forth, rest on arms of ash,
that sulks and storm, snoop earshot with panache.

Chimneys coerce smoke signals Earth delivers,
lucidity sends message of hard shivers.

I have nothing left to ask except these words:
I wish grief would turn into wittier birds.

The poinsettia is cumbrous with flower clusters.

Children lie quietly on yellow buds.

The quite shoots are strong,
beyond the age-old path,
where wild oats whistle,
pale amid rustles
of corn husks

Blue water falls over the rock.
The red cardinal's moans soft.
A shepherd follows the sun,
that rolls from the winter hill.

Indigo moments see spirit.
A timid deer emerges
from the forest edge,
while the old rings out,
and new rings peaceful.

More devout the meaning,
cold and winter in lonely rooms;
bright footsteps glisten holly green.

Soft rattle of an open window; seas
of abandoned on the hill
brings tears to eyes.

Memories of legends,
stilled times,
souls grown lucid
hold joyous people,
the colorful days
of Christmas.

Sunset's last gasp
of sun swells into my room,
Light flashes showy top shelf
of Depression glass.

So, I can't quite tell
if it's the sun or lamp.
The kind of glow
where one has to posture back
to study the whole picture.
December bright!

Outhouse duty calls,
but this captivates me;
an ocular statement
of winter grasps sight;
like all beautiful things
it will vanish soon.
Everyone seems
to talk about December.

Store windows scream brisk,
and red "Christmas is here!"
stuffed with wrapping paper,
bows and cardboard cutouts.
Santa in overhauls drinks apple cider.

Do all love this season as much as I do?

Refreshing feel
of the wind,
cool but not cold,
when I push past
the needle of one hundred M.P.H.,
down hills and fly over speed bumps.

Unbridled sky illuminates my mustang.
On these days joy and peace elapse
into space. Things plentiful
in life are undefined cares.
Memories of last year's season
lie too still.

Mock-orange trees cry out rapture.
I accept this December won't be the same,
but it will be just as lovely.

I promised myself it would.
Baked gingerbread cookies smell,
and the air is shivery when I stand up.

The fact I notice these things is a good sign.

Once he swore love to me,
and the face he wore was mine,
left me to remain poetry's slattern.
Views past crow's feet and slashed
wishes my love would melt his hate.

People say what does not kill you makes you strong.
I am entering winter,
and know the long road home.

The no pass zones in the road,
the curves past Highway 302.
Ten miles downhill.
You have left.

My dreams are about the snow.

Verbose drifts,
manners being cold,
done up in frozen rain.

I do not remember how it falls,
and I am what people call brave,
and I am what people call able.

White, pure, and falling,

irrepressibly falling.

What am I? A slattern
that would snatch a married man,
from his wife's arms,
take what's already taken.

Beyond the dreams that echo snow in me,
my fiery soul builds his face in flakes,
kiss all points, as if his eyes could see
beyond me, past today, tomorrow, next year.

If he's so able
to quickly melt
the memory of me,
then, we were never
falling together,
just a whirlwind.

Out at the fork of the river,
thick with trees,
brush and blueberries,
we'd fill empty tin buckets
in the hand carved green canoe.

(Remember how the paddles
sliced the water sideways
on the facade water is
something to push against?)

My sister always wanted to be the hill,
sway predisposition on this soul
under the rays, beyond the river,
pressed back against me on my lap.

Our old home place was creosol brown.
White trellis stood surrounded by sweet

peas and puddles.

I remember stretches belly-down,
small and clay dirt's chill, shifts
of warmth against worn-wood porch,
stares down the tea-colored river,
seeing the green canoe, plunged
off the end years ago,
river clamshells,
hard and heavy,
halves stuck tight
against water.

Water-spiders dance,
cross reflection,
over river's edge
to the other bank,
where similar children play.

Smells distinctive
of pine tar and possum,
smoke from pot-bellied stoves,
and hard lye soap pushed
into small hands by Mother
with orders to wash in the branch.

Only, one time in her life,
my sister's quiet enough
to hear sharp-skinned hawks
call to splash-flipping fishes,
calm enough to hear sand wash
against the river and its spill out
drag on painted sand.

The cochlear snail shells she pushed
into pockets
to count at home led her

to forget exact days,
and beginnings.

Every memory swims mature riverbank.

She never stood in Carolina,
pushed up from river's edge
through the soles of her feet,
a poised cardinal in the shade
of our home place.

Instead I became
the hill off these banks
in Lexington,
pushed up from the bottom
of the mud-colored South Edisto,
surrounded by someone else's kin.

But, I tell her as we splash flip
in this water below a wood-worn porch,
pushed up with my arms against where
she falls sun-warm in my lap:
water is nothing to push against.

Swollen clouds roll past the hill,
weak sun and wind howl
cold and loud, hurl the trees,
and swirled the leaves fall
in the street, not earthbound.

But the baby bird so small descends fast,
from cold that is sky,
never heeds land that stops and starts,
listens to a teacher that whistles.
The baby bird knows this is school.

Leaves that skitter in streets,

Wind tossed and ripped from sky,
crickets that sing and cry,
bring sweet music to dwindle and die.

Foolish hearts think they can fly.

This bird is small and brown with white down,
and frightened black eyes.
I would touch him but
he stutters and starts.

I would cup this small dream
in my hand, and feel
the fluttering beat of the sky.

But the teacher knows this is school
and her lesson is calling me down.

Even as leaves take wind, pull
the farthest blown bough,
and clouds, loud and rolling,
sky-high and bound for sea,
the sun is ever falling.

And when brown bird, brave, tender
of heart, finds wings, and follows
my eyes ascend
to his home that is sky.

I know the secret of expanded space,
as I know the pull of ground.

It's winter in South Carolina and Bullet's is quiet at
five.
The clock is pushed back tense in the wrong
direction,
and the wind blows hard at the door.

My daughter pulls her quilt,
and I press my face to her cheek in affection.
The clock moves forward in rapid rotation.
Time has sprung in some hurried progression.

A lifetime unwinds in unpretentious generations.
Withered wheat is the color of her hair.
Beside me, her face has taken on the harmony of dreams
and she is unaware.

She is dressed in careful clothes,
a nightcap covering,
braided rosettes in golden-red hair,
my greenness, I've wrapped around her,
and in dream's death I've tightly bound her.

Her freckles are those displaced mica glitters
from some rock gathered long ago.
She must know the mountains through her hands.
She doesn't realize her hair is the hue of fields
and far reaching trees.

in fall when the land is the most
before it dies I'll be older,
and she'll still be fifteen.

Me, that much farther from mountain-blown skies.
For her the mountains will always be lands,
and leaves that have evolved to death
for the trees and flutter
to the ground.

In this state I once overlooked
how she's now constrained,
and her heart will not pound

with the mountains or the wind
that in empty spaces retreat.

But, when she wakes in her life,
and in time she will know,
it will all be enough until she turns
to me with those eyes
with their memory of my life.

Sometimes a small mountain valley
can span twenty years temperance
with mica dirt and glittery crust
on the surface.

We wade through dawn past lost seagulls
to see a moon full for how many days
rising, setting,
and sun brilliant flashbacks after midnight,
barefoot in creek beds halfway expecting
the depth to rock the surface?

Space of twenty years time tames wild
out of the wind,
as the memories come
to me tentatively,

Sometimes I have to dig for river clams
in his waters where he scatters shard,
unceremonious scraps of colored glass
off the end of the bank, and wait
for the sun, and sometimes nothing.

I crouch in the mud, stare
hard with my heart,

as if I could pound
into memory

the coarse muck,
between my fingers,

the sun over water,
uprooted clams

from another age,
ancient crustacean,

harbored under glass,
as if shelving ruins

brought them closer.
Land locked today,

like another age
of being away,

and parking lot
seagulls that aren't

even that much
wheel and cry

over my concrete bed.
I'm as much out of place,
Uprooted, as these lost gulls,
and sometimes wonder if my creek

cries as clearly from there,
as it does from here.

Sometimes ladybirds migrate and die frozen,
scatter in the mud, frozen at the end
of the bank.

Him with his arms uplift, scatters glass the color
of blood, faith, promises me water, and the rasp
of time rubs smooth sharp edges.

I want to be a poem with meter,
but able to hold my beat in secret,
darkness like the rush
of a pulse, so real

palpitations hit the electric air.
Real as dusky depths of the hunted,
oyster's perfect snow-white pearl,
trapped in sand below rainbow's hue

of white prescient of the moment
where each line melds a reader's view.
Shape afire, hot pea gravel poetry
burns bare soles and every bone,
in one body at a time.

Seductive and thick as that captured breath
whispered in smoky reading rooms.
Illusive the casual eye seeks
the peak and big blue surface,
for eagles and hawks against bridled sky,
as much to what this body draws coming
in vain seduction of reality.

Never to peer through these blue eyes
past some deceptive stereotype
life, the face I wouldn't recognize
crawls out of my skin, again
never to follow colloquial poets,
elevated from frenzied passion,
pushing heartfelt existence,
more so, than the poet's paper,
pen squeezed against all limits.

I want to be a poem,
freely versed on how to be,
a rhymed couplet,
meant to be as whole and round,
and real on a read page,
as the shape and taste
of your tongue.

When birdsong paints the weald,
to gather up hushed sweet smells
of softwood and he comes,
song will erect Horse Shoe Cove.

This is a place canoes lie secure,
nimbus will rise between us,
on the path to spring,
at edge of the pasture,

and frog croons to cricket sounds,
on their pedestal near the pond.
I'll be there, wherever there is,
watchful, and waiting.

I'm slicked back ready
to scat, the kind of chick
that nicknames the toms,
has a mean hip swing,
paints the Moulin rouge.

Smoke is always in my reach,
neon green eyes.
This momma mouths words
to verse and when I get it wrong
throws backside to the air.

It's what you'd call
instrumental breakdown.
Forget balance sandwiched
between psychopath and therapy.

I'm a porno on fast forward,
prom queen, sweet as ice cream
lives at the carnival,
dives in buckets of chlorine,
desires a date, disposable love,
something referred to as our song.

I'm the disco with full beams on,
wants to bang some big Ben,
wants to breathe fire.
My love is a mad sunflower
that forgets fragments
of sun in the silence.
His radiant atmosphere
of light hides
my drained conscience,
a wing splinters in air,
gropes the mire;

filled with myself—
gorged—
I discover my essence.
In the astonished image
of water, a tumble
of angels fall
of their own accord
in pure delight.

Essence has nothing
but a whitened face,
half sunken, already,
an agonized laugh
in miasma sheets,

Mournful canticle
of the sea—
more aftertaste
of salt or cumulus,
than lonely haste
of foam pursue.

Nevertheless—paradox—constrains.

The rigor of the glass
clarifies it,
the water forms.

In the glass it sits,
sinks deep and builds,
attains bitter age
of silence,
and the graceful repose
of a child's smile.

In death deflowers
yesteryears
of disbanded birds.

In crystal snares it strangles,
there, as in the water
of a mirror,
it recognizes itself;
bound there,
drop with drop, the trope
of foam withers in throat.

What intense nakedness
of water dreams
in iridescent sphere,
and sings thirst for rigid ice?

But, a visionary glass—that—swells,
like a ripe grainy star
flames brave promise,
like a heart mends happiness,
and promptly yields
to the water.

Essence is a round filmy flower,
a dart that achieves height,
and a window to joyful cry

that smolders independence
oppressed by white shackles!

Hear these groans rattle
from fixed skeleton,
hear the past,
and what is to come.

Hear the present,
and the sound
of coming and going,
life's roulette wheel,

the dried-prune cadavers
of birds that speak tongues,
eyes of abandonment,
and thirsting voice.

Roger's body is the world,
belly a square of sun,
shoulder performs rites,
and my glances wrap him like weeds,

he's a town the sea assaults,
a stretch of parapet split
in two halves the color of coffee,
a field of sand, rocks and birds,

dressed in the hue of my desire,
I travel his deep-sea eyes,
the phoenix burns in those flames,
and he's a thousand suns, sprays ocean.
We lose ourselves in white tribes,
essence sets sail, and we misplace
our names and drift in the indigo,
where the world swings tranquil.
Love is anguish, a question,
a luminous doubt suspended;

it's a wish to know the whole of you,
and a fear of finally knowing it.
Love is a secret rage,
an icy and diabolic pride.
Love is a mute, green envy,
and a subtle and shining greed.
Love is an unaccustomed luxury
and a voracious gluttony, always empty.
But to love is also to close our eyes,
to let dreams march into our bodies
and sails without a course, itinerant;
because love in the close up is torpor.
It is paralyzed, mute, and gasping
like a heart between two spasms.
If I keep him imprisoned,
and caress him and hide him;
if I feed him in the depths
of my most intimate wound,
if my death gives him his life
and my frenzy such delights,
what will become of me Death,
when I must leave this world,
untying this angled knot,
you too will have to leave me?
Daydreams are with a pirate,
his map and boat,
race onward with hope
to find the jeweled chest.

Lost in lazy moments,
beneath beady parrot eyes
of a one-legged woman's first mate,
the milk in my coffee dribbles
onto the hopscotch floor.

I loom larger than the growing drifts;
a sea of sparkle. The sand is cold
and I don't let river water touch me.

In Lexington County we listen
to constant inner voices peripatetic,
midnight urges of Lake Murray.

In the morning the same chants race
the burning November leaves;
a Carolina autumn's latent splendor.

Seasons are the most elusive deals.
Every time the weather changes,
there's a weatherman turning up.

Nearby, springs jog a stream of thoughts:
Fingers point crooked and bent
moving swift as day speeds to night.

The air around me stills, joins worlds in unison.
Realize all must run to the fast lanes
of nakedness and cold,

yet, my mind awakens to buds
of Mexican petunias and fragrance,
the skin of the ripened apple's perfume.

Quietly, I rest offhand and knee-jerky,
reverently, stand temperate and alive,
miss the bleakness of borders, and think.

The rain slows away from the tempest;
swings over the woody ridge; swishes
in the gorge. The air is filled with atoms
of condensed vapor.

Precipitation hems a grave in clay earth,
sparkles rain on monkey grass nearby.
The mindset carved in arms jars memory.
It's autumn once more in the Carolinas;

balm fragrantly scents under the sun.
Climatic areas touch fall's chaos,
press drops against solitary breasts,
buttocks gallivant the undulant forest.

Thunder cracks over the sand hills,
lightning trembles, almost invisible.
Clouds puff dame's rocket pallor,
peddle the sunning splendor.

Opaque bodies of the bellied clouds
brush over the undersexed hours.
Time slips away, as downpours gush.
The pilfered flashes fuse and disappear;

fractals outline fact and vision.
Fission can only be one of love realized.
Sleep stirs me on the sand-filled floor.
I've grown old in this lost afternoon,

bent by rain-floods of a teetering mind.
A blue bird erupts from crimson stamens
to fly away as insanity rocks intoxicated
to fresh smells of stir-crazy jubilation.

How I love the slight,
swiftly beating heart
of the red-legged thrush,
singing in this peach grove.

I'm aloof, in the knowledge
of what cannot be or change.

Fields speak.
Masses bend over whispers –
grab life that shifts stone.
Even the shutters swing,

windows jar, screen doors slap.

The memories draw decades past
when a child's braids blew cool night air
and chased fireflies.

I'm tattooed with stains my apron hides,
and saggy heart meanders toward forks.
Paths lead to other rain-blanketed fields.
Sparklers sizzle and rival the noise;
cotton bowls slurp sopped.

It's the season in between; cool air dithers
calls of the cicadas hike steep, drifts snow,
floats out split ends of mountaintops.
Icicles articulate in this mind melt.
It seems like life's passing quickly.

Bones snap and bare toes pop,
pull at my umbrella.

A strangle catches heaven's tears.
The reach for small miracles festers
festivals of longing tells me ample room
still remains in places where hope blooms.

I hang to sober days,
peep between the gray and ochre,
watch the silver queens stand.

Both fight their ground and know
the battle's won for this season,
if only, to hold back the ears of hunger.

Fodder is the winter beast, cobs
decorate the fields, my spirit rises;
blue eyes bat the crow's return.

My desire is to cast off old clothes,
rise like a belly dancer's navel
in seduction against the tasseled gray.

Clouds mass, freezing rain falls,
touches knowledge
of how superbly loving I am.

The rising sun sinks today;
clouds watch me tangle trees.

Magnolia leaves
flat with brown edges,
like Mexican acrobats
who suddenly flip across
telephone lines.
These leaves persist,
blushing atoms
of chlorophyll and molder
grow into tamers
of simple country girl.

I glow in southern sky.
Blue-green eyes bat butterflies,
endure this Judgment Day,

Clouds start mass,
shame lust and stench;
sea breezes grasp my spirit.

I think of Armageddon,
as the sun shatters,
waves fragments one moment,
glitters like jewels the next.

Antimatter obscures the sea, opaque and flat,

lead-colored; yet again, minutes later,
the sun reemerges, strikes the waves
in scintillating nerve-like patterns,
hypnotic to the eye.

The planet revolves around my head
like a moon of pensive waters.
Thick rainbow oil slicks ribbon the air,
painting plasma color whispers spells
to birth foreknown future.

Wild urbanity erupts, shapes its grottoes
and carves the worm hole coast
to labyrinths involved as longing,
elaborate as the force of ceremonious religion,
and stars spin candy-cotton bloody
to deliver the sky trawler.

We hover naked,
as wind snakes the stallion.
Eyes are black and liquid.
Clouds of ebony drape their bodies,
and night. Starry graves open,
a constellation sprouts
beings that flee into lifeless distance.

Clumpy clouds graze salmon-colored;
oxen float on blue sunless sky.
Below fields of porcelain newborns sing.

On flat fluency the indifferent planet loops,
but humans remain confused,
mish-mashed in judgment,
conjoined as Siamese twins.

Their perpetual orb opens and inside,
other worlds spin. Inanimate and real

faces not committed to memory
utter alien sound as they grasp for hearts.

Sounds heard circle us to short-circuitry –
No wild guesses touch the backdrop of stars.
Spastically, I empathize.

We must talk about everything
according to nature,
slice through the crap we conceive.

Don't just give me glimpses of sex,
middle-of-the-road chitchat
and hot apple cider,
give me substance and pithy centers.

I long for the spin of planets,
to be the concentric circle of force
strung out to the last fermata.

Under the sun of gypsies
fireballs spray, billows glow,
turn intimate,
portray this hour.

Lonely, in this soft flee of madness
I survive in a galaxy and swing
on sandy shores of waterless seas.

The woodman makes daily trips
down our road, past the pumpkin trailer
in his pickup truck.

A sure-fire way to tell the ghoulish season
fast approaches. Neighbors cover yards,
try to fight off frost. So many enter October
without jobs, beating their fired wings

with food stamps and no money.

This is how fall burns.

I hang to night swinging on my porch,
eyes cross-dressing the full moon
that peeps between gray and ochre clouds.
It holds onto life in such high places.
like we all seem to do.

Blackbeard must surely live,
as the stars gather like sirens
ready to make landfall after chills
in the air have left them moonstruck.

The notion of a pirate and a star ship
of ladies tickles my brain
given his larcenous soul.
Only a fool could believe
they were banding together
to bury stolen treasure.

It is ball season and I cry foul.
My posture is one posed,
maybe even like a person
from the Medici circle arresting
Michelangelo's attention.

He, too, had a love of literature,
learning the lesser art form of poetry.
David, his human statue stands drowsy
awaits mud bath. My desire is to break
free from the stonewalls that imprison me.

I'm not a fan of autumn,
but will share my red delicious apple.
We can throw our core to slutty pears

that paint yellow promises,
the promise nothing ends.

Thanksgiving with turkeys is next.

He watched the pouncy shadows play.
Their beauty became a silent movie
held an audience of one,
awestruck by mystery.

I see the wild sea and a happy child
born without permission.
She inches her fingers into my heart,
deposes my dreams with laughter.

stalks clean panes and snowball blossom.
She'd never visited where snow fell
in summer, and the grass grows square.

I'm frightened
by the sorrow
of an escapee.

Let's Play Ball.

Fresh grass, fans,
tornado dirt,
Sweat jewels,
Hotdogs,
Tobacco spitting,
Players, dugout,
Balls, bats, gloves,
Team uniforms,
Bird shit
Umpires.
The crowd inhales last drag
of joints, fatigue and slump.

They all fall into place.
Batter's ball rushes hind catcher.
His hand and feet pace high-flying mimic.

Coach claps and stomps,
and umpire tada's a call.
Cow ants crawl the mound,
cry mantras foul.
Pelion is a big barn,
dots pirates and babes.
Scenes of being set up,
spectacular and wind-jammed
spotlight fields.

Today tree frogs croon rain;
I circle the calendar in songs
about a full moon coming,

how wedded memories sway antique,
jiggly sunsets stir desire.

Each pleat of the vacant sky paints
tortured longing.
The lukewarm rock crosses emptiness,
intersects where
the sun folds back red.

returns cocoons,
melts the scenery,
melts heart
as poetry dives from tongues.
This is the place I fly to,
when other poets play tag,
touching the inward part
of my being.

Devoid light calls

from aberrant landscapes,
misplaced lovers,
the absent fireflies in flight.

It's almost too early for coffee,
and the sun glares at me,
as it pulls itself over the sill,
but I'm happy.

Roger makes an omelet,
stands in the kitchen,
whistles in his boxer shorts,
his testicles swing in perfect time.

It's going to be a great day.
It's already a great morning,
and the first egg he broke
was a double-yolk.

The rest of the eggs are common,
as is the milk, and the margarine,
and just when he reaches for an onion
to liven things up, three mice appear
from behind the toaster.

They are dressed like Latino bandits,
and they demand the cheese.
They wear little sombreros,
carry little pistols,
and the one in the middle
has its whiskers waxed
into a handlebar mustache.

As we stand there pondering
the intricate mechanics
of their tiny guns,
they inch across the counter,

and repeat their demands.
No one moves.

The only sound is the slow suck
of hot water through coffee grains.
Just then the toaster pops up,
and we smell burnt toast.

Morning sun bangs windows,
the planks buckle, tilt me
like the only good pea in a pod.
I run tips along crystal edges to hear music.

Space takes over our room.
Color rises from flowers
down the hall, yellows the ceiling thin,
lets in the sky and creosote floats on floors.

My husband remains whitewashed in sheets
wrapped up in noises beyond the wall.

Last time this happened my body
was useless as his mind.

Even the neighboring preacher's wife
became restless.

No one ever told me
how sweet milkweed smells.
I get to find out for myself,
like a toddler turns flips
in dewy deep grass,
emerging hive covered.

Emptiness shakes its wet fist,
spreads out the holler
where rabid hounds hump,

and ghost voices echo
falling down
only, to shoot up sand hills.

Life is weathered and wild;
wild buds sleep –
everything and one abides these days.

The chickens bunch against cold
between straw, shelves sag heavy
under light bulbs. Slide down slick.
Bald eyes beg for feed.
My hands grab pellets
and throw right then left.

The wind whistles,
then whoosh I'm lifted,
right out the door,
landing knees first,
scrambling,
plugging ears with fingers,
reach to cover eyes.

The tin skirts, walls crash, a tornado
of flying feathers surround
the chicken coop
that takes a final moan,
surrenders
to the crowing afternoon.

Each morning is make-believe.
I'm an owl nailed to southern sky,
pretending to live.

The metal roof weeps tears
only, I see it as the devil,
he beats his wife.

Seldom brightness rises thin,
and still above rainy sphere.

Love can also be quiet and sober,
hold a silence that time without end
cannot depress.

With a trembling certainty
day-by-day death slides
its umbral scythe
over the lustrous albedo
of each hour.

With a long liquid sigh,
the hammered scene stops.
I watch other birds fly
down the highway.

The sky lives in a shell
where the sea comes.
Like me the beach sun has packed
its umbrellas, and strayed
over sandy hills.

My ears sound out walls;
cold plaster shapes
umbilical cords.

The study of design
listens for kicks,
and I remember
a kind of music.

The walls sing:

Paint me, Paint me.
The color Peony Frost licks
like a tongue in the ear.

I'm now the oiled girl.
An onlooker might swear
they'd seen a rebirth.

My inner child tries to speak
in a voice past a whisper,
but is doused by the brown
life shouts of a chance crisper;

defeat of any defense one might bear,
exodus of a soul astray in midday.
So, love finally speaks in a murmur,
about all the unimportant things
that cause disarray in a happy life.

As shadows pronounce hushed tones,
thwarted burdens turn our bones
held high with the massive dross,
and dazed life escapes giddy.

Real life utters not in pitied whispers,
a raspy gasp against our ears.
Doubt enters empty heart,
breathes away all remains of cheer.

And a collective conscious commands,
speaks in a shout and screams
that ruins our cherished dreams,
and dictates what life is all about.

Deep in the drifts
of truth and lies and memory,
I reach beyond my grip for purity.
Sagacity of time leads me,
near discovery of truth.

This journey leads to wonder
if the answers I seek
are neither past nor present.
Sagacity of time tells me;
the answers I seek will not deliver purity.

This journey wears not a path to answers,
but broaches a greater inquiry.
Sagacity of time assures me;
I'm close to the right questions.

Tell me how you've planned to go.
Tell me how you're tired of dust
filled roads, sand
from which it came.

Tell me how you long for pure
dry places, flat and green,
not the blues and browns
of counted days silence hangs.

Eyes seldom ever meet
our abandoned muddy soles.
Stones outside cover tracks;
regret lingers not forgotten.

How does it feel to run
barefoot in the rain
away from puddle rings
to shelter stilled by the sun?

I am singing full songs
of love to God above,
words that till the laughter,
heavens convey gardens
of comprehensive set out thoughts
being something we've all shared
the same redolent but promising air.

One solitary spirit gazes
past silent thickets,
raises pug nose to hills so high.
Rising breath sighs thanking God,
as pockets full of posy fly.

Treasures simple that a heart has found
views nature's silhouette high above ground.
Oh Lord, please listen to all the cries,
as one fallen give thanks for life in world
that hurries fast, tumbling down!

Drifters on the edge of silence,
half afraid, all alone
waiting for a sign.
The deep parts
of our hearts
swoon sullen,
as the tide swells.

And, all the tide
that lapped our lives
seems ocean bound.
Isles of inland dreams leap
vernal season shells sand,
mixing particles;
siren-like melodies peer
with quiet laughs,
and fade along the shore,
lapse between the piers
and the unknown green.

Suddenly, songs sung splash
the purpose of life saying grace:

And, since it came out of nowhere
we couldn't hold it.

It was not ours to hold.
It was not anyone's.
It was a windstorm.
And nobody owns the wind,

Sun-filled land glistens invisible
in yellow space and magic,
fragrant from the oversight
of two cliffs,
(dancers in hilly breeze)
running point to point,
yet near enough
to run rough rocky
pursuits and listen
to excursions of soul
echo, echo, echo.

I can tell in diligent delay
a candid future waits.

Roger and I sit in the garden;
we've surrendered,
watch the chicken hawks circle,
and I ask if he remembers how
to spell scarecrow.

Eyes corner my peer,
where I rest framed
in metal.

It's an Indian summer evening,
the scent of muscadine
and roses fill the air;
an event I'd refer too
as a lover's night.

His tight eyes, focus,
and confusion sprouts his brow,

and he asks, "What?"
"Scarecrow" I repeat,
see the denim shirt,
and plaid checks reflect.

"How do you spell it?"
Roger sighs, looks back
at the chick hawk, and replies,
"Use the dictionary."
And I think of something
he once told me.
Spelling bees were for ugly girls.

Nibbles at my naked toes
through the pompons stroll,
as the sun above so sweet
warms grass-speckled feet,
and beneath a tree you stop,
and stare, and see me
in my sashes bare.

Flashes of me fly away,
and heaven burst its seams
for me to stay.

Bridges left to cross
were but a dream,
leaving ailerons
capable of flight,
suchlike,
a splendid sound.

Water drawn-out in motion,
and fountain drinks whisk by
never to touch the sand hills.

If only I could fly,
this form would always be
in the sky.

Music whispers and twists
nippy cornflower blue.
Distant figures in the open sky glimpse;
glitter of the eternal lie silent,
occupies joy in airy dalliance,
and where what is about us scatters
leaves only ourselves to find slivers
of starlight that pierces
the hearts of men.

There should be
a place where no tears fall,
sorrows are forgotten
and pain heeds no call,

the soul untroubled rests
like a windless sea,
where the depth is clear
for pure eyes to see,

an extended hand is drawn near
beyond reproach,
and kindness conquers fear,
where gentleness is not feigned,

a place where the heart is at peace,
with the light of truth will never cease.

There life could be seen
as from a hilly height
and winged spirit
would soar in effortless flight.

All mans creations pass away
and nothing compares
to the singular rare beauty
of a flower which spring bears.

There should be a time
when men's hopes are fulfilled,
where home is found,
the seed planted in the soil tilled,

there in silence and prayer
to God will we'll seek,
the care that is sown,
and the good, which he'll reap.

The clouds and rain will come,
but not the rain of despair
the night will follow day,
as it's always done
and we'll sleep without a care.

Wind will come,
shake the chaff,
leave the kernel sound,
and the season will pass,
while life lies secret
in the ground.

Day to darkness
cite stars at night,
emotional chimera
evenings artificial intelligence
filters out dull effervescence
shines without a sun,
only a sign.

Rich tobacco souls,
like candles glow

evening's dawn from skies carapace,
lucent from memories taunted face,
silent gleams sent home
streak like the shooting star
evenings dim amid the race,
fireworks from the pulsar's dance
frolic up the spirits
of wit honor others for messages sent.

Honest mirth for they that drain
wellborn fire from the influx train,
likeness from a painted sky
to higher matters ornately fly,
with such sighs the respite seek
a view of the moon so meek.

Wrestled by thoughts of a mere
word painter strive to endear
my face to landmark of his heart.
Measured by a melancholy sky
erupts fusillade from cloudburst darts,
across immaculate chaste night
lining a half moon face lights,
begs for relief from a mercy seat
one gold cherubim hoped to defeat.

Evil wills of analytical engine screens down,
dazzles darkness reflected from a gown,
kills conversations with the night,
and evening's spirit takes flight.

Wild white daisies
of thought permit seed
to be tamed,
so they may be thrust
in fields of love and eternity.

Fragrant innocence exists
in meadows dispense
by gusts of winds,
or bird skill.

Landscapes remain created
by God's hand, flower painted.
This is the Promised Land
where hope dwells.

We begin to dance,
slow at first,
visions wrap muse,
mysteriously transformed,
as air itself shimmers.

Eye colored ocean waves
and glistens in sunlight;
scales tone tinged to twilight.

Sandy floor deep drifts white hair,
and ebony nights
beach combed tides
spin waves and scales concurrently.

Free-falling flows rock back and forth
continuing to will their mark
against sandy floor.

Softly, the sparkling here splashes there;
turned cartwheels abandon starfish.
Snail's pace withdraws running away
coming again only to leave more;
spawned beauty held within.

Naked hunger drives us here
in scant winds and light,

arranges its distance
before us like kisses we wish for,
at sunset of a tangerine horizon,
behind us restless,
with mountain strands,
on an indifferent day,
where some silhouettes miss possibilities,
and fail to risk themselves
from cosmic sweeps in telltale lands,
flights away from reality
dance silently in mute parades.

It seems last night's sleep lasted
a hundred years.
I herald dawn, a renewed life.
Jubilantly, the rooster crows.

Outside someone has stolen the sun.
I search and search
so I can bring it back.

The phoenix soars above,
sun perched its shoulders,
falls off into the swamp.

I learn to endure trials,
return to bed
After more sleep I'll be able
to glimpse the found rays
of an emerged dawn light,
painting blue flaws.

All around me lie riches,
gentle breezes, golden trees,
peacocks and crystal streams.
Magic of calm water,
the beauty of surprise,
the hum of tree frogs
cast their spells.

Has life ever been so uncomplicated?

As morning sun peeks,
blues cast over me,
and scatter shadows elsewhere.

Glimpses of thousands of afternoon sleep
mirror my eyes.
My spirit's wistful,
small reminder that time moves on,
and even a perfect summer cannot last forever.
Why is it always arresting –
sun's low saffron flicker,
and golden highlights to day?

Why is life ephemeral,
and my expression enigmatic?

Wheat fields slice hair,
and seem,
as if spun on a turned wheel
through purple clouds.

Likewise, I'm taken back
in this once-upon-a-time world,
where nothing is strident,
or jarring, but perfection becomes
bittersweet reminders, earthly joys
fleet like the seasons.

Sun darts to top of endless cornrows,
flashes hue and orange races barn.
Even the cow ants dock
in roadside ditches
to watch.   I admit how I stare
at the red tribes,
all standing on their heads,
rump to air.

I suppose from the beginning
my eyes were meant to accept shock,
constant surprise,
and shaken again and again,
even more amazed.

I need all of this,
because when I return
to that place beyond death
I'll learn the meaning of certainty.

My inner child tries to speak
in a voice past a whisper,
but is doused by the brown
life shouts of a chance crisper;
defeat of any defense one might bear,
exodus of a soul astray in midday.

So, love finally speaks in a whisper,
about all the unimportant things
that cause disarray in a happy life.
As shadows pronounce hushed tones,
thwarted burdens turn our bones
held high with the massive dross,
and dazed life escapes giddy.

Real life utters not in pitied whispers,
rasping gasping against our ears.
Doubt enters emptied hearts
breathing away all remains of cheer.
And a collective conscious that commands,
does speak to us all in a shout
in screams that ruin our cherished dreams,
and dictates what life is all about.

Deep in the gorges of truth and lies and memory
I reach beyond my grip for purity.
Sagacity of time leads me;
near discovery of truth.
This journey leads to wonder if the answers
I seek are neither past nor present.
Sagacity of time tells me;
the answers I seek will not deliver purity.
This journey wears not a path to answers,
but broaches a greater inquiry.
Sagacity of time assures me;
I am closing in on the right questions.

Somewhere down the road,
I hope you hold me in your memories,
cherished, as I'll remember you,
even if it treads my soul a lifetime.
Today, tomorrow, laughter, cheer,
and sorrow exits,
the highway is like a river,
low and high,
and I live with love
knowing you will enjoy the ride.

Tread on silver wings unbroken,
walks on life's threads
of pearls bring blinding splendor,
and the bluest hue;
as I watch you leave on a rainbow so bright,
promises of a future with pure delight
knows fate rides in on surprises
that is not within our outreach of sight.

Rain cradles sprayed pools;
washouts of sunless song
on mountain carrel,
its motion laughs back.

Lookout from vast stretches;
one can stand stone's throw
more than what is safe
without being near.

Tell me how you've planned to go.
Tell me how you're tired of dust
filled loam roads; clay
from which it came.

Tell me how you long for pure
dry places, flat and green,
not the blues and browns
of counted days silence hangs.

Eyes seldom ever meet
our muddy soles abandoned.
Stones outside cover tracks;
regret lingers not forgotten.

How does it feel to run
barefoot in the rain
away from puddle rings
to shelter stilled by the sun?

Birthed gulfs
of melodious music wave passion
to other troubadours,
that wrote and did not listen,
as sound levels glisten,
and energy rays rose
to leave weather tantrums
to pass and go
for days the notes
bobbed robin sings.

Titillated tones balance
his articulation superb,
rings rhythmic say-so
brings freedom,
and releases muse.

Beats built on a chorus line burst
open nature cries for the blues,
and pop pop melodies.

Tension between forms caress wicked,
whims hold captive,
and red daubers hit hard,
lock in and restrain robin's cupola.
Gated to be different,
sometimes with indifference,
Vibrations blow off again and again,
asking,

So softly! Surprise takes over treaded steps,
a barefoot earliness for the second, no minute.
Pitched against time
the bobbed robin's song he sings,
calls me tells me over again and again
asking,

So softly! To leave weather tantrums
to pass and go.

Swings hung from sunbeams
and enchanted mornings lull,
as life bursts open surprise.
Wild beats lure tick-tocks impatient,
scampers nature's clock charged.

April's view of time is strength mixed passion,
spirited eyes, luminous life of fascination.

Rife queries reason invented or otherwise,
looks downward as hyacinths bloom bright,
and revelation lies within white majesty beds,
alongside holy lilies that silhouette paradise.

Tired soul blends with blades of grass,
blows past seeds, thought-filled grief,
and limbs stretch slowly upward toward the sky.
Lines strings the birdsong kite flying high,
while whippy clouds dance midair.
I sing songs full of love to God above,
words that till the laughter heavens convey,
gardens of comprehensive set out thoughts
being something we've all shared:
the same redolent but promised air.

Treasures simple that a heart has found
views nature's silhouette high above ground.
Oh Lord, please listen to all the cries,
as one fallen give thanks for life in world
that hurries fast, tumbling down.

I kept saying to myself, "To be really crazy
is to believe in something you desperately want,
not thinking about the aftermath."

Is cloudy news to be shared with all the world?

Such as all the verses one muse might spout
in-enraptured performance,
and undaunted expression.

I imagine one should entertain the secrets,
like many, before them and utter
solace to those ripe and beautiful eyes
that captures this muse.

I can tell in diligent delay
a candid future waits identity
never tempting early flight.
Sight so ripe is in your eyes,
as I see a moon of reflection,
luminous and brimful of mystery
with passions abound,
sweeping, stealing every veiled secret
I have ever known.
I tell you, we cannot let our souls die,
as peace imparts this night of beauty,
God spins this sphere a little while longer
before we all share the greatest
of mysteries beyond life.

Tuned piano music gallops
the heavy splay of paint.
Incandescence moves sphere
in epicurean sprawl.
Everything enchants us.

The night swells and quivers
on the last notes,
and we fall like moths
against the heated light.
I sigh to the magical moon.
Dreams flash on and off,
like myriad
lights, pale or rouged faces, tired,
yet sustained by weary excitement.
I'd marry the stars tonight.

The dawn strips, flings its will,
beats me to a new day.
Shoulders slump in sandy contempt.
Piano keys cross ground,
breaks the window,

adorns my thongs,
slingshots me into function.

At Thanksgiving the supper table glitters laughter,
confuses placement of guests,
the curious turn to the captain's chair.
We wait and wait for his eye patch
to drop off.

All balance on the edge
of the furniture,
and talk of all subjects
except the main gossip.

When the fatal bird arrives,
I watch neurotic guests with wonder.
The unknown elevates into importance,
and an orgy of social behavior erupts.

Stuffing from the turkey's rump
become a pattern of faces.
When the affair ends
there's a weird delusion that strains were over
at last, at least, until next year.

I picture the future
as an ocean of sand,
long level stretches
of I-20 scurry fast,
under a red roof of tin.

My family thinks I'm a bit eccentric.
How the suspicious pursues my moments!

My schoolteacher daughter's smile extends
from ear to ear, lips project.
Her beady greens peep
over the sweep of her nose.

I read her thoughts,
and how she transforms the barest episode
into a thing of curves and contour.

The afternoon suns a new sensation,
strolls color and mellows our age.
Stilled music, infinitely sorrowful.
The entrance of night is a moving -
picture show.

I've photographed the moment.

South Carolina is like a hand up my skirt.
I can't move towards it or away from it.

It's postcard perfect.

Almost.

The first day of winter - 12-21-2007

We're enclosed within a Faraday cage,
touched by brittle bones. Nerve ends
chase round indoor existence,
want to be outside.

Long panes look over fields of wild onions
holding down turned-over earth. Icicles over
heart melt like nearby duck ponds.
This slow trickle of thaw
opens the hunting season.

We're not ready to be mistaken
as flight risks, birds that try
to keep in touch, sewing back threads
of torn wings, eager they'll hold --
not split.

Hunters are giddy with drink;
statically charged electric fields.
It's a play place, performers gun down
jolts of another kind.

On a day of rain and ragweed pulses throb,
seek asylum between marshlands.
Camouflage watches decoys scatter,
crisscrossed mirages of fog rise and fall.

A gloved orange hand signals.
Shots are discharged. This gyro of doom
and blood needs to know spring
is holding room for us in new flyways.

December is the peak time
of heartbreak or happiness.
Yellow jackets bury bodies,
sucked up by the sand.
Television screams about scams,
and (sap)suckers.
Like the owl curiosity peeks awake.
Holidays bring sadness to most.
Even to me.
Three minutes after 8:00 a.m. Sunday
I hopped in my car,
spun the hill and stopped.
Smoke poured from the front bumper.
Four stabbed tires.
Attacks like this are personal.

The local police informed us
they'd be on lookout for tire stabbers,
but there's only three or four on a shift in town,
and this allows for a very limited search.
Besides they've other things pressing:

hassle the Mexicans for example,
or sit in speed traps,
and wait for teenagers
to burn by setting fires
in adrenaline zones

On a merry morning
when unimaginable hordes
of smoke has rushed
past thought perils poise
in the shady woods,
where I can't fly.

The smoky stink assails the senses first,
Then the rasping alarm quiets.

A blue bird erupts from crimson stamens
to fly away as insanity rocks intoxicated
to fresh smells of stir-crazy jubilation.

Fifty plus becomes shadow
rising in droves,
and drone overwhelms heart's song.
Roger sits singing his refrain before diving
into darkness that creeps close.

I've heard this before,
but it was nearing midnight then,
and the overcast night garbled his song's version.

Even then, I was a loony-acting warbler,
breaking out like fractal equations,
knowing there's genetic logic involved here.

Mid morning worries return,
hum pitched accusations nearby,
and my skin feels the sting
of a hundred fire ants.
But this is winter,
and isn't possible.

The sun flattens to a blade.
Cold-hearted the crimped car
glints at my fill of the feast
distorted and distinguished.

Peacocky crowns hang over my head,
brilliant blue/green/red plumage marks,
iridescent yellow eyelike spots.

Parched
mouth
eager
for spring rain
licks my cracked lips, stares
unblinking into the sun's eyes.
He does not discriminate, grants me bias freely;
singes ground, burns the brook beds dry.
We swallow dust, share
our car's pain.
Neither
quench
soaked.

Soft melodies of madness walk up
in front of me.
We've grown old in this moment.

This scene bends my mind, a solitary ghost,
pleads defiant to our ragged spirits,
emulates this simple dread.

I resume peace in pieces,
pull myself together.

This morning chorus dims,
yet, I remain to listen for dusk's chorus as well.
It might as well be wails of a sad violin.

Planted in sand a spectrum of gray arrives
with sunrise. Daybreak is still dark,
but a faint glow of hope drops like dew.

Roger has slept,
but it hasn't changed his cadence.

Swelling with words,
December's notes flitter, pine
away from a sprightly tone.

Feel the cold, a ticklish chill behind the breastbone.
Air faintly vibrates.
Darkness gathers itself up and falls on us.

I feel like a lost bird looking for a new place
to land. I'm not just a lost bird
but a barred owl swamp-bound.

This past year or so I've heard sorrow in the
branches.
Limbs break and the sound boomerangs
between my ears.

I'm often crushed by the decency of other people
who had almost nothing themselves;
at times I've felt their kindnesses so forcefully,
I'd thought it would destroy the delicate inner part of
me.

My nephew was one of these people, so cool.
With his jean jacket,
black work boots,
black beard,
and memorable eyebrows --
thick black eyebrows that bowed slightly forward.
Not like Dr. Spock or any Treckies.
No, more like a country rock god,
maybe a counterculture revolutionary
booming confident, and as he grinned
his cheeks dimpled,
visible in spite of his beard.

I've always been a labor of love,
one a person has to work with constantly,
but not him, he was just a pleasing person.

The concept of his death alarms me so
my brain blinks weak,
and thoughts go slack-jawed.
He'd just started settling,
readapting to the real world.
Do you know how many things have to go wrong
before this happens?

I remember
how the email slapped me backward,
spun me off my feet,
slammed my ass into the floor.
In an instant I was seized
by a glimpse of God
with his hands outstretched to Heaven.

Through tears and rain I drove,
watched the visual distortion,
a subtle warning of things to come.

My face flushes a paler shade of rose,
eyes gleam and tear,
when I think of him,
and how I prayed for God to take me instead.

What more can a fifty plus person offer
to a world she's seen the best of?

At this moment I think of my Uncle Jim
who could wiggle his ears,
and called me his ugly duckling.
He'd let me pet his white dog with one ringed eye.
My head swivels in the past's direction,
and I feel thankful there's no mirror
to reflect the expression in my eyes.

This heart is suddenly out of breath --
it skips beats. I wanted so much more for him,
for him to fall in love with someone great looking,
brilliant, maybe a belly dancer or a poet.

Nothing like I did,
fall for a geriatric sport's fan
who thinks erotic massage
involves a tube of Ben-Gay.

I float away a whole afternoon thinking about it.
Peace, a silent sound so intense
causes the bones in my chest to pound.

My nephew's voice rises from the ground,
surrounds this tormented soul
toe-struggling with death, and whispers,
"See ya."

People have to keep going because
they don't know when something awe-inspiring
is going to happen.

For a year plus nothing in me has wanted to get up,
wanted to move past this memory and work.
I think of how work is even mandatory for all
who pass away.

The dead organize the seasons.
All depends on them.

In May, the dead unearth worms,
crack baby birds from their shells,
poke the croaks from toads.

The children who die make play
of their work,
blow ladybugs from weed to weed,
revive fields with their somersaults.
They thump the yellow jackets
and fling them out to pollinate flowers.

The old ones who die prompt roosters to crow,
discharges dawn each morning,
directs the wind,
and times the tides,
become midwives to animals in labor,
strokes the dying sun's head
until rays spread pink and orange,
then summon the moon to rise.

The burly ones who die drive rivers
downstream and upstream,
maintain the sky's motion,
stitch the clouds,
green the grass,
tug it taller,
grab tree trunks,
and stretch them skyward.

The loving ones that die kiss every bloom,
pinch shoots until they burst open, stunned.
The shy ones who die string spider webs,
barely visible.

There's a job for all the dead,
on any given day.

Unless, of course, they are annoyed,
and then they call the yellow jackets away
so nothing will flower.

When they are upset,
the dead arrest the rain,
chain it to their belt loops,
and laugh when soil cracks.

But for now it is spring.
The season is simple.
The season is new.
We are all content today.

Rising crescendo lifts spirit,
and a rosy salmon sky displays
a spectacular idea.

We'll move. Again.
Exuberance is mind boggling,
and daylight performs a sonata.
Volumes increase, then the concert halts.
Wind pushes me inside,
and the search begins.

I hunt Roger to tell him of my epiphany.
He's on top of the house, dancing a jig
on the peak of our A-Frame,

barefoot on shoddy shingles,
and he's spinning his arms,
stirring the air.

Life in Leesville has come to an end.
Roger and I will dart.

We're two ruby-throated hummingbirds
looking for sugar water.
Soon we will be safe under a new roof,
snug in the comfort of newfound safety.
Hopefully, hordes will quit droning.

We're running away.
The desire drives me to tell our oldest off.
That it is a wonder God let her know us
for as long as he did.

And I might have put my son in situations
he didn't like, but I'm only human.

As far as my middle child,
I love her for being so good.
Then there is my baby.
She could run a third world country
with her pinky,
and stop the storms
from gathering.

Air grows still but the rain stops.
My tongue's thick
as a drug addict that overdoses.
Trembles start,
and anger is bigger than anything in me.

Even a dog that gets the shit beat out of it
doesn't bite the hand that feeds it.

I've waited all week for the sun to come,
but it doesn't arrive.
No sun, no family, no voices.
The landscape's strange.
Children seem to have a knack
of finding your dearest possession
and destroying it.

In my case it's my heart.
You can't spend your life living for somebody else.
I'm not an antique, maybe a limited edition,
but even Roger and I have pride.

Our new address is white and big,
columns on the front porch.
It reminds me of a birthday cake.
I know it can withstand any storm.

We'll huddle in our new home,
peer out the picture window,
and watch storms pass us by.

Even then I'll want to hug the ground,
listen to the earth suck up the rain.
Tree arms will beat the panes
like the fists of a robber.

I'm not so sure we'll be in a safer place.
There'll be noise all around,
sounds of a train.

Maybe the devil will paint a tornado,
and head it our way.

Sometimes something comes along,
tears your roots right out

of the ground you stand,
and that's when you know
you've been planted too long.

Because of the past – the winter –
our future arrives earlier than spring.
I look at it as a Christmas blessing.

Direct sunlight will be extinguished
by the larger tree's leaves,
catch our energy,
and we will be driven
to newer and more phenomenal growth.
Grass even grows in this new postcard.

I live on the edge once again,
spring up like an exotic flower,
and squints are on high beam.

Roger is also a plant
marked with green,
juggling resources.

Everything starts jaded,
then buds or spikes into bloom.

One can be a seed,
and be in wait
or either race toward the light.

I wonder how many are shade lovers,
and how many actually hurry
with little time for dillydallying.
After all, we are human,
not black widows waiting
to mate and kill.

Pale pink memories drop heavy blossoms,
and black squirrels flash fangs thistle long.
Flights of rabid bats send me to bed.

We'll learn to feel like spring again;
the climax of having the right to rebirth.

It seems ground is always rocky.
I know things have to change.
It's just that I'm lonelier than most,
and after all this time,
the only certainty I have is my writing.

I imagine I see Chris riding a Harley,
a belly-dancing poet in tow.

Roger's teeth catch light
the way a diamond does,
and I'm driving again –
Unrestrained.

e Author: Sarah Picklesimer Wilson

... Appalachian ... She ... poems, has blue ink for blood, and is double jointed. In addition ... of writing, reading, ... and is an avid quilter ... nature ... She lives ... and sincerely hopes ... her books.

About the Author: Sarah Picklesimer Wilson

Sarah is a native Appalachian from North Carolina. She wears aprons with watermelon pockets, has blue ink for blood, and is double jointed. In addition she enjoys all forms of writing, reading, painting, and is an avid quilter, which evolves from her native roots. She lives with passion and sincerely hopes you enjoy reading her books.

Lightning Source UK Ltd.
Milton Keynes UK
12 January 2010

148487UK00001B/193/P